THE JAGUAR TEMPLE

THE JAGUAR TEMPLE

& Other Stories

Julie Keith

Cover art by Seymour Segal.
Cover design by Ramez Rabbat.
Photograph of Julie Keith by Diane Deruchie.

Acknowledgments
Some of these stories have been previously published in the following magazines and anthologies: "The Jaguar Temple" in *Canadian Fiction Magazine*; "Falling" in *Fiddlehead*, *Souvenirs: New English Fiction from Quebec*, and *32 Degrees*; "Rabbits" in *event*; "Karl's Story" in *event*.

The author wishes to offer special thanks to Terence Byrnes and to Michael Harris.

Published with the assistance of The Canada Council.
Printed and bound in Canada by Imprimerie d'Edition Marquis Ltée.

Dépôt légal, Bibliothèque nationale du Québec and the
National Library of Canada.

Canadian Cataloguing in Publication Data

Keith, Julie Houghton, 1940–
The jaguar temple

ISBN 0-921833-38-5

I. Title.

PS8571.E4458J34 1994 C813' .54 C94-900791-9
PR9199.3.K44J34 1994

NuAge Editions, P.O. Box 8, Station E
Montréal, Québec, H2T 3A5

for Gena

Contents

FALLING

The bowl of flowers sits askew on a pile of magazines. As though someone has abandoned it there, thinks Lil, and some time ago too. The daffodils have frayed into brown shreds. The crimson tulips are spread wide to reveal surprisingly opulent centres, the purple so dark it looks black. Beautiful really, only not like tulips. Not what you'd expect.

Except for the tulips, and that abstract painting on the far wall, the room is done in shades of cream and yellow, the palest, most boring yellow Lil can imagine. In the quarter hour since she and Edward arrived, she has studied every inanimate object in the room...the furniture, the fabrics, the walls...everything, in fact, except the faces around her. Especially the face of Edward's first wife. Joanna's dislike (and it must be dislike) presses like a dead weight on Lil. She wants to jump to her feet every minute and start screaming.

Phrases such as "sheer expediency" and "the next election or else" have occasionally reached her, but she has no idea what the men are talking about. It's awful to be hated, she thinks now, for perhaps the third time, glancing again at the ravelled edges of the daffodils. Awful. If only someone had cleared those dead ones out, added water...if only this, if only that...

A duet of male laughter signals the success of the conversation, and Lil casts an involuntary glance at their host. Colin has kind eyes. That's one thing. And his curly brown beard gives him the look of a minister. Quite unlike Edward's fierce, clean-shaven jaw. Colin, in fact, looks altogether a gentler animal, the sort who might find himself at least a little bit on Lil's side. Besides, doesn't it make sense that Joanna would have chosen a softer, more contemplative character as her second husband? Why risk getting hurt a second time?

Lil's eyes flick to Edward, then back to Colin. No, they really don't look alike. What is it then about Colin that reminds her of Edward? Something in his knowledgeable laugh? The quick, positive way they both speak? Is it possible that Colin, like Edward, prefers at all times to run the show? He does have kind eyes though…

"Sounds like a double-edged sword to me!"

Colin's remark startles Lil. What can he mean? But the men are both smiling. And now, Colin leans back in his chair and takes a large swallow from his glass. The wine represents his newest find at the liquor commission…a merlot, if Lil got it right.

Colin explained all this about the wine in the first cavernous moments of the visit. Australian, he informed them, while pouring out four big goblets, each so full he seemed to be making some further assertion.

"Exactly," Edward is replying. "It won't matter what reason they give. The deed is done." The two men nod at each other, and then Edward too takes a large swallow of wine.

Daring to glance at their hostess, Lil sees that her eyes are flickering ominously. Grey, tired-looking eyes. They travel from Colin, gently pompous behind the furry beard, to Edward's vigorous features, and then drop away. Getting to her feet Joanna moves with her heavy swaying walk toward the kitchen.

As if she can't stand Edward's presence, thinks Lil. She blinks her own, very large, very made-up eyes (getting ready to come here, she kept adding mascara). Or maybe it's their dual presence. Not one more instant of the recombinant couple.

But no. A moment later Joanna is back with a tray of cheese and bunches of fresh, dripping watercress. She steps around a pile of newspapers and places her burden on the coffee table. At no time do her eyes lift to glance at Lil, who is seated directly facing the tray.

Lil would like to jump backwards over the sofa. "What beautiful watercress," she cries. "Oh, cheese! Oh, I'm so hungry!" Sitting up straight, she snatches a nugget of cheese and pops it into her mouth.

Joanna says merely in her soft, slow voice, "Watercress grows here." She crosses the room and sits again. Lil slumps back. She will be stuck here in Joanna's living room forever.

"No crackers?" complains Colin putting down his wine and peering over at the coffee table.

"We're out of them," Joanna says.

"Then what about that pumpernickel I bought the other day?" he asks. Joanna shrugs and then nods.

Colin turns his head and draws in a breath. "Teddy," he calls. "Teddy! Will you come in here a minute?"

The boy appears almost immediately in the doorway. He is nearly ten, cheerful, slightly impatient. Lil gives him a quick smile and then glances at Edward. He too is smiling at Teddy. Something brown has smeared the boy's cheek...peanut butter maybe, or chocolate. The tail of his shirt hangs well below his sweater. Nonetheless he is the only person present who looks at ease. Colin instructs him to bring the package of bread. "On a cutting board. Don't forget the knife..."

"And hold the knife point down," adds Joanna. "If you fall..."

The boy looks amused at their fussing. "I will, I will," he interrupts.

They can hear his running footsteps, the banging of drawers and cabinets, and a moment later he is back. He slides the board with bread and knife on it in between the cheese tray and the precarious bowl of flowers. "Okay?" he challenges them and stands back.

Edward, who has been watching, lifts his hand abruptly. "Come here," he orders. The boy smiles as though this is some special joke.

As he sidles near, Edward reaches out and makes a grab for him. The boy dances back, then comes forward again suddenly to thrust his arms around the man's neck. In turn, big tweed arms enfold almost the whole of the boy's narrow body. And for what seems a long moment, the two hug. Then Edward's arms drop down. Meticulously he tucks in the errant shirt tail. He pats the boy's rear and then, as if inspecting his person, turns him full around, still in the circle of his arms. "Now then..." He grips the boy between his knees, takes out a handkerchief and rubs off the brown smear.

"There," he says and grins at the boy. "I can see your face."

"Okay, Daddy. Okay, okay," says Teddy, ducking his head. He squirms in the vise of his father's knees, but he too is grinning. Released a moment later, he remains standing by Edward's chair, one hand on the arm. His eyes, skipping from one grown-up to another, taking in every move, are as eager as his father's. His mouth turns up at the corners with the same optimistic curve.

Lil thinks of him as a small, elfin Edward. He has been easy for her to love on this account—he resembles his father so greatly—but, of course, he has other traits as well. Different traits. Oh, my, she thinks suddenly. For Teddy's soft, pale hair must certainly come from Joanna. His wide forehead too, now that she thinks of it. And what else? Many things no doubt. Oh, what a price. Poor Edward. What an awful price. And leaning forward, by reflex almost, Lil takes a piece of the bread and holds it up in front of her face, as if to hide the glimmer of triumph she cannot help but feel.

Colin, who has decided at this point that all is going well, gets up and crosses to the coffee table. Smiling benevolently at Lil—what an awkward-looking girl—he proceeds to arrange the cheese and bread into miniature sandwiches which he then offers around the group, with varying results.

Lil actually bounces in her seat. "Oh, thank you," she cries, "I mean...no, thank you, I have some...I can reach it if I want..." and she sinks down again into the sofa cushions. Teddy wrinkles his nose as the tray passes. Edward takes a piece of cheese, leaving the bare slice of bread on the tray. Joanna, with the merest shake of her head, closes her eyes as the tray approaches.

His duty done, Colin replaces the tray on the coffee table appropriates two of the sandwiches for himself, and returns to his chair. Now that the guests have been supplied, he happily eats a sandwich. For one thing, he is hungry, and besides, he loves a sharp cheddar...nothing better, except that it does sting his tongue. He has told Joanna this many times—that for him the taste of cheese is too strong without the alleviating blandness of crackers or bread—but she forgets. Not that she means to be indifferent, he has decided. It's simply that individual tastes do not seem important to her.

Now, settling the second sandwich on the arm of his chair, he takes another large swallow of the wine. Full-bodied for a merlot. Even with the cheese. He nods to himself but does not say anything for fear of sounding pompous. (He knows he can overdo this sort of thing.) He does, however, like to serve good wine. Full-bodied if possible. And he does like to take care of people. Throughout the visit, in fact, he has been keeping a solicitous eye on Joanna; it is he who has urged her to take this step, a sort of normalization of relations. Also, he admits to himself, he is guilty of curiosity. The former husband, Edward, appears at the house from time to time, collecting or delivering Teddy. But the second wife, this Lil, has remained offstage, an outline merely, an unseen character in the drama. Until now. And now he is surprised. This second wife, the vamp, the villainess of many tales, is so ordinary looking. Long and awkward of body, unkempt of hair, no more than pretty, she sprawls on the sofa, her legs jammed under the coffee table. She is plucking crumbs of the bread off her sweater with angular fingers. If asked, Colin would say she looks skittish, those big whisky-coloured eyes. Certainly not glamorous. And no poise either...none of Joanna's pleasing languor, the stillness that hovers about her person. For Colin, wherever Joanna sits, wherever she stands, is the quietest place in the room. By contrast, Lil's corner of the sofa seems positively aquiver. Of course, the girl is probably a bit ill at ease. She has barely spoken except to produce the burst of compliments about the cheese, which she hasn't touched since.

So where then, thinks Colin, munching his way through his second sandwich, where is the Cleopatra he has been awaiting? The scene-stealer par excellence? For the implication has always been that the theft of Edward was accomplished by means of a physical attraction no less than magical. And yet, he does not doubt the truth of Joanna's perception. The image of "the other woman," the stories of betrayal and suffering through the long affair, have dominated too many late night conversations for Colin not to believe in the history of treachery, in the reality of the pain endured by his wife. They made her life a sham, treated her to any sort of lie. That's the kind of thing she says when the memory takes hold. Edward was there, but he wasn't, and she, Joanna, never figured it out. She just worried. She kept thinking if she got pregnant again... Whenever she reaches this point, her voice slows and she stares straight ahead. Colin knows then to put his arms around her.

He glances over at her now and nods to himself. The need is still there. For isn't it true that in the small, light eyes of his wife, in the blueish tint of her eyelids and the soft bruised look of her mouth which is not now smiling, the suggestion of martyrdom remains?

She is replying to some remark of Edward's. At the same time, Colin sees that Lil is dragging herself up into a more presentable position. Her corner of the sofa seems to provide no leg room, and the coffee table with its burden of magazines, bread board, flowers, and cheese is still jammed up against her knees. But at least, thinks Colin (who likes his women to be womanly), she can no longer be described as sprawling, she does have one elbow neatly propped on the pillow beside her.

Lil has decided, in fact, that it's time she make another foray into the conversation. For whatever the larger truth, she has no call to take on the role of guilty party in this gathering. Besides, I'm much younger, she reassures herself. As though guilt can accrue only with age.

The cheese and watercress topic having been exhausted, could she ask about Teddy's school—isn't there some soccer game or school play in the offing?—or about the garden? These over-extended flowers must have come from somewhere. But the flowers are really too decrepit to be mentioned, and the subject of Teddy is a cliff-edge. Is there nothing safe to offer? She glances around without taking in much—at best she could say that no one is either weeping or snarling—and is tempted to announce that the whole visit is a bloody farce.

It's exhilarating to explode like this from time to time. Besides, such unpredictable behaviour is one of the things that attracted Edward in the first place. Lil knows this. Her manic reactions and energetic triumphs, even her downfalls, still excite him. And she is still entirely capable of making a scene just to get his attention. But here...? Inwardly, she shakes her head. Here, the consequences for him are too great. Edward has, now and seemingly for all time, a precious hostage in the enemy camp.

"Such lovely flowers!" The high-pitched declaration startles them all. Lil as much as anyone. She has heard her own voice with genuine surprise. The bravery of it enchants her. Surely Edward has taken notice. "I saw the garden coming in," she adds by way of explanation and makes a gesture that nearly knocks over her goblet. "I mean outside...you grow them?" She addresses this to Joanna, who tips her head slowly to one side as though she is regarding someone demented. "I mean..." Lil chokes back a sharp desire to laugh. "I mean," she says carefully, "Are you the one who does the gardening?"

Joanna consents to nod. "The soil here is good," she says quietly. "And spring flowers are easy of course. Later on..." She shrugs. "Working I don't have much time..." Her voice is a dead calm. Lil sees Colin stiffen in his chair. The "working" remark must be a loaded one. But Joanna is going on. "Teddy helps me," she says, and Colin leans back again.

"That's nice," says Lil. She looks over at Teddy and then at Edward, who does not see her glance. His eyes appear to be fixed somewhere above Joanna's head. Lil's eyes move to the painting that hangs on the wall behind Joanna. And abruptly she remembers. It must be the one he has talked about, the one he chose for its colours—deep stormy blue, slashes of red—the one Joanna wouldn't give back. From time to time he still conjures up anger over the refusal. The painting was his, and indeed, thinks Lil, it does seem out of place in this pallid room. Too rich, too strident. She glances back at Edward hoping to catch his attention. Did he think back then what she is thinking now? And she decides, yes. Of course. The simile is so obvious. Here in Joanna's house, the painting is like an escape route. No less. It is like a window through the pale wall.

Colin glances at Lil glancing at Edward and decides there is no question—his own wife is much more attractive. Edward must have been out of his mind. Joanna's dove colouring, the slowness of her movements compared to this jerky boy-woman... He sees Lil drain her glass and realizes that his own and Edward's glasses are nearly empty as well. His caretaking, host's nature twitches. However, he has promised Joanna. He will not offer refills. Enough tolerance and civilized behaviour being enough. She does not, quite naturally, want them here all afternoon, and since Colin is the sort who hates to let his guests go, he has been made to promise.

But still he feels chagrined as Edward and Lil lock eyes. Do they sense the hospitality withdrawn? Probably. At any rate they are agreeing with little nods that the time has come. Rising, Edward places his hand on Teddy's head as though to memorize the shape of his crown. Lil gets uncertainly to her feet. She glances around, searching for her purse perhaps, wondering if she should clear away any of the glasses or anything else. Once or twice she shifts her weight. Her movements seem unstable, unpredictable even, especially compared to Joanna's smooth rolling walk as she leads Edward and Teddy out of the room.

Only Colin is left watching a moment later when Lil abruptly pivots, her face fresh with relief, and grabs up her purse from behind the sofa pillow. And it is then, at this moment so close to the end of the visit, that he sees the sudden grace of her. Like a running animal, he thinks staring at the unfolding body. She seems to be leaping as she crosses the room. Out of control. Her knee has jarred the coffee table, her shoulder smacked hard against the doorframe. There is a sense that she may carom off the face of the earth. As she swings around into the hall, he feels a hunter's urge to chase her, to corner her and make the confrontation last. Eye to eye he would face her down. Her fear, if it is fear, would make him strong.

And yet in the moment he takes to catch up to her, the illusion has disappeared. She is uttering a too effusive thank-you, then fumbling her way out the door after the others, putting one hand on the stair railing to steady herself, starting down the stairs. As he is watching, she turns her head and glances back, and he is totally unprepared for the smile that streaks across her face. A brilliant, almost hysterical smile. He can hear the ring of laughter behind that smile. And the look she flings at him now, a look clearly meant for him alone, is both so full of guilt and so confident of his forgiveness that he thinks she would be able literally to get away with murder.

He is still standing there stunned when she misses her footing at the bottom of the flagstone steps and stumbles into his wife's border of daffodils. And without warning the whole of his heart rushes out to her. He wants to leap down the stairs and help her, to right with his own hands that long, kneeling body. And standing there in the wake of his wife's pained cry and Edward's exclamation, forbidding himself to move a muscle, Colin imagines with absolute clarity just exactly how it would be to fall in love with her.

THE JADE CAT

Elizabeth pauses at the lookout. The view, almost the whole of the harbour and the city on the near side of the island, still dazzles her. Lately, she has stopped often to savour it. Because she knows their time here is growing short. And because there is something addictive about such an offering, such beauty. Whether from the island or from Kowloon, to face the harbour is to stare down and down. Think of San Francisco, think of Vancouver, Elizabeth has said in her postcards. And make the hills steeper. Ten, fifteen degrees steeper, until you can hardly believe the whole glittering impossible city won't go sliding into the water.

Now she accelerates and wrenches the car into the hairpin turn. The next curve affords another fabulous view, but Elizabeth is too busy to look. Feet pressed on the clutch and brake, she almost stands on them, as though she personally were holding the car against the side of the mountain. The houses up here are all new. A development which has made some enterprising Chinese entrepreneur rich. Three hundred million is the figure they have heard. The entrance sign is in Chinese and English. Hong Lok Yuen—The Healthy and Happy Garden. Place names here in China are often sweet and slightly comical; sometimes they are beautiful, the sun moon lake, the silver leaf garden. Rodney's company owns this house. It leases an apartment on the island too, but the house is for men with wives when they come out for the obligatory year. Sometimes it is longer, but for Elizabeth and Rodney it will be just this one year. The company needs him back in Montreal.

And the year has been perfect. The things left behind—her Masters in clinical psychology, her lover who is dumber but nicer than her husband and nearly as tall, the running club and the squash league—all of it can wait a year. The exile has been a relief, almost a pleasure in itself, the sense of unreality here, of being out of time, which will of course begin to tick again a couple of months from now when they return to Canada. Here they go to the races, a scene in which the sport is entirely subservient to a display of frenzied gambling. Here they play tennis at a friend's club, since squash is for men only. At home she would be wild about such an exclusion. Here it doesn't matter. None of it matters, and besides, there is always the view.

Elizabeth parks and jams on the brake. She gets out of the car and leans back into it for the first load of packages. The maid, the older one who is always eager to help, will come rushing down in another minute. Elizabeth finds this obsequiousness embarrassing, that she, tall and strong, should be waited upon by the tiny, tea-coloured old lady. Trying to forestall some of this service, Elizabeth makes a point of carrying the packages up the steeper part of the steps, almost to the door. The yellow steps crisscross twice, zippering up what passes as their front garden but is in fact only a small, straggling hedge of flowering bushes that more or less lines the steps. Elizabeth has made a point of not learning their names, these bushes with the big cerise flowers that bloom and fall in a day. She hates gardening. It is all the English women here talk about. No, that's not true. They talk about servants and schools and how soon they will travel back to beloved England. The Canadians and the Americans are better. Though at first stunned by the heat, the humidity that in summer presses down like death itself, they rally. They're not quite so conceited, Elizabeth has decided. Some of them try to learn Chinese. She herself studies Mandarin down at the university. She knows about sixty characters now. She cannot, however, talk to the maids, who speak only the language of Canton.

Up the first flight, she feels her heart rate pick up. She is still fit in spite of much less exercise, no place to run. The maid has appeared at the top of the stairs and is hurrying down to relieve Elizabeth. There goes the white man's burden, she thinks, handing over the packages. She is starting back down when Mr. Chen's chauffeur-driven Datsun wheels around the final bend into the Healthy and Happy Garden. The top of a round, black head barely shows in the rear window as the Datsun passes Elizabeth and pulls into the driveway of the house next door. Mr. Chen is their neighbour. He is unfailingly pleasant and polite, fluent in a mad sort of English that has no articles, definite or indefinite, and is all expressed in the present tense. "Street very high here. You drive fast-fast, climb hill..." The Datsun is large, heavy, ominously silent. Mr.

Chen is rumoured to have underworld connections. His car, she is sure, doesn't whine in the steep curves the way hers does.

"Hello." She waves and smiles. Mr. Chen bows. Elizabeth bows back. It is impossible to resist the impulse.

They have never seen the inside of the Chen house, she and Rodney. They never will. Chinese society is closed. Everyone has told them this, how Hong Kong is a series of parallel worlds, how gaps unbridgeable lie between them.

At the beginning Elizabeth tried, as her American friends tell her they too have tried. "Come to dinner," she said one afternoon to Mrs. Chen. They were standing in the street at the time. Mrs. Chen was a small, lacquered woman, younger by far than Mr. Chen. She looked very surprised just then, but surprised in a neutral way, not as if Elizabeth had said something remarkable, but as if there had been a flash of light or a sudden loud noise. Then she shooed her little boys toward the steps.

The two came scampering directly toward Elizabeth. She could see the ironed pleats in their matching red shorts, the stitched cuffs, the designer insignias on their miniature red and white rugby shirts. The elder, who was perhaps five or six years old, ducked his head politely as he passed. But the littler boy appeared not to notice her presence at all. Hustling to catch up with his brother, he actually lurched into her leg and then stumbled and fell at her feet.

Bending to collect him, she felt immensely pale and tall. A foreign guardian angel bending to rescue the little Chinese boy. And what a very little boy he was. Flickering and fragile in her hands, his cowlicky hair a crown of black flames, his arms no more than willow wands in the soft jersey. Yet, as she set him on his feet, he sprang strongly from her grasp and flew toward the stairs. His wild dash continued to the first landing. Then, as suddenly, there he was peering back down at her through the railing, his small face split into an impudent grin. She gave him a quick wave, but already he was scrambling up the next flight of yellow stairs.

Mrs. Chen gazed after him with anxious eyes. She still had not moved from where she stood, and she looked, in her white linen suit and platform sandals, both perfect and untouchable.

"Next Wednesday," said Elizabeth turning to her. "Or Thursday. What about Thursday?" Mrs. Chen stopped gazing. She blinked as though Elizabeth had wakened her. Then she nodded her head and smiled. The smile made her eyes disappear. The oval green stones at her ears quivered. She said nothing. "Yes?" persisted Elizabeth.

Mrs. Chen smiled some more. Her poppy-coloured mouth slowly closed, then opened, then closed and opened again. "May...be..." The syllables stood apart like separate words.

"With the Chinese, yes means maybe," said Rodney that night. "Maybe means no." He was cleaning his pipe and paused to glance up at her.

"Well, it's maddening," replied Elizabeth, who had been stalking around the living room while she pondered the incident in the street. "Their little boy must have bones like a bird's," she added. She could still feel the elfin arms in her grasp. "Tiny, tiny...I picked him up."

"They're a very small people," said Rodney. "The southern Chinese are a very small people." He set his pipe on the table beside him and took a swallow of his drink. Then he laughed and shook his head. "They're nuts too, you know. The staff brought in the Fung Shui man again today, for that new office we're setting up. We had to move the sofa to an inside wall; the joss wasn't good..." He shook his head again. "Speaking of small, he was the smallest guy you ever saw, about three feet tall, and he had a ton of incense with him. He said there were monsters in the board room."

"You'd think she'd know *I* wasn't a monster," said Elizabeth grumpily. "I mean, I was nice to him. I picked him up." Rodney shrugged then. The Chens were out of reach, for whatever reasons of cultural disjunction. Elizabeth knew that. Rodney was right. There was nothing to do but give it up.

Now as she continues her descent, kicking a fallen pink flower out of her path, Mr. Chen has reached his own front door, which is almost as high up as Elizabeth's. The door slams a second later. Is the interior filled with the smell of incense and dark, heavy furniture, carved wooden cabinets and chests, inlaid tables, enamelled brass vases more beautiful than jewels? Elizabeth can imagine all this. She has seen these wares in the thousands of shops that line the angled streets of the city and cluster under the great hotels that rise along the harbour. The objects are beautiful, mysterious. Elizabeth cannot conceive of owning such things. As it happens, she hasn't shopped at all, a fact remarkable in a city that is a shopper's paradise. Nothing? Nothing? Her friends say she is crazy. When will she ever have such an opportunity again? The prices! Everything so cheap. "Wery chip," say the shopkeepers, standing in the doorways, holding out the silk, the pearls, the watches with games and computers built miraculously into their flat shells. But Elizabeth says no and no again.

She wants to move unencumbered. For here in Hong Kong, the streets themselves are her desire. With Ted at her side she wanders Kowloon, threading through the perpetual crowd, peering eagerly down every alley and around every corner, breathing in the smell which is sometimes incense, sometimes fish, sometimes just heat and humidity and bodies. Above their heads thickets of neon signs, red and yellow Chinese characters, sway like branches and leaves, blocking out half the sky. In the first months when she knew no Chinese, the characters were designs, beautiful arcane symbols. Now she searches among them for the few she knows, so the effect is different though still exotic.

Ted loves these meanderings, says he loves her. Instinctively she knows that the more magical she finds Hong Kong, the more star-struck she is, the more he will love her. Always before she has picked tall, handsome specimens, fastidiously making her choice as though she meant to breed by them or to make some statement about her own taste. But Ted is short, stocky, and grey-haired, though younger than she. His hair curls in tight spirals all over his head and down the back of his neck in two parallel smudges. He says his hair is something else since he came to Hong Kong. He can't do a thing with it. His glasses are thick and dark-framed so that each time when he takes them off, his large, kind eyes surprise her. Each time. There is a kind of pause each time, a moment when everything hovers, the possibilities are uncountable. She feels a shiver of fear then—what might happen if she were to love him back—until he takes her into his arms, and safe again she closes her eyes inside his protective embrace.

Since the top of his head comes up only to her eyes, since he stomps along the frantic streets looking pleased and vaguely surprised at his good fortune in having her beside him, she has never worried about being seen with him. Though they have met acquaintances, even mutual friends, no gossip has floated through their crowd. Elizabeth would know if there were talk. People's behaviour would show it. Sudden silences, eyes that drop and are then resolutely raised to confront one's own. She knows how it is. Perhaps it is Ted's air of innocent enjoyment that protects them, even more than their physical disparity. At any rate she knows, with the certainty of instinct, that they are safe.

Coming into Hong Kong on the last flight from Taipei, she and Rodney had hardly bothered to stare out the window. It was dark, and they were so tired, both of them, that they had run out of thoughts. Surely it couldn't matter what sight they glimpsed first, some disconnected view from the plane. But they had gasped over it, literally. Behind them a woman stifled a cry. The plane swept down the harbour between the great tall buildings, actually below their summits. She and Rodney had peered out the plane's window right into balconies, seen directly into the lit windows of apartment buildings. Feeling Rodney lean across her, press against her breast as he looked out, she succumbed for a moment to hope. The two of them here in this exotic city, extracted from the old life, perhaps...But a glance at Rodney's profile, the lift of his eyebrow, the satisfied thrust of his lips—he was nodding to himself; probably someone had told him about the flight approach—this single glance chilled her. No, the adventure here would belong to the city itself, to a world of people whose rough black hair was the antithesis of her own, whose eyes hid unknowable meaning behind their epicanthus folds.

The first week there were cocktail parties. The English-speaking expatriots had their own world, established and apart, but for Elizabeth and Rodney there was a whole crowd of temporary exiles like themselves. They were greeted with open arms and trays of drinks. New blood. She met Ted at the second party. Someone at the company had chartered the Rothschild junk to cruise down the islands for an evening. Cold wine and beer were served as they churned through the misty night. In the distance a line of lights marked the edge of the land. Hills, blacker than the sky, rose up against the clouds. There was even a moon shining through the mist. With the warm, wet air blowing through her hair, Elizabeth had sat staring out across the water. She felt placid as a child, perfectly content with whatever might blow out of the mist. The atmosphere was magical, mysterious, yet friendly.

Ted sat down beside her and offered to share his beer since she appeared to have nothing to drink. He asked her the usual questions. When they had come out? How long would they stay and where? What did they think of the life? And then, when she turned to face him, he held up his hand.

"Stop," he ordered and, reaching over, tipped her head away from him. "There." He traced the line of her profile with his finger—forehead, nose, mouth and chin—and sent her heart racing. "There," he said again. "It's perfect when you're gazing off like that. I thought so." His hand cupped her chin for a second and then dropped so that she could turn and stare at him. Her heart was still thudding. "You don't see all that many perfect things," he was explaining quite seriously. "At least not perfect living things. Are you nice too?"

"No," said Elizabeth.

He nodded—she could see the faint light move up and down his face—and then after a moment remarked, as though continuing their conversation, that she would love Hong Kong.

"And love you too, I suppose," said Elizabeth in the same harsh voice.

"I hope so," he told her.

When they reached the floating restaurant a little while later, he handed her up off the boat. Returned her. Her fingers felt weak in his hand, and then she was standing on the pier and Rodney was calling to her, and she was peering at her hand to see...to see what?

It should have been impossible. He was short and a bit stout. He looked like Henry Kissinger if he looked like anyone. She would never have wanted to have his children. But she went on being bemused by him. Almost fascinated. He was such a surprise. Such a character really. He didn't appear to follow any of the rules. He invoked none of the usual conventions, took none of the usual steps. He was, in a way, absurd.

"We'll get married," he informed her. It sounded like a child's declaration, and he made it, the first time, so soon after they began to see each other that she didn't even believe him.

"It's just my face," she said, fishing but cutting off the nonsense too. She has liked being beautiful these last years. It was a way of offering something, of satisfying people, without actually having to do anything.

Ted admitted he loved to look at her. He said he didn't know why he loved her though; the point was he did. He was waiting for her to love him too. The issue was simple. Marriage was their destiny, the natural end to their affair. "You'll have to keep your shoes on at the wedding," he informed her and covered her bare feet with his own. "Terrible," he said affectionately, putting his arms around her, and she felt that even her feet, white and bony as fish skeletons, were appealing in his eyes. "Our wedding," he said over and over with perfect seriousness. He seemed utterly confident that one day this would all come about.

He didn't press her to tell Rodney. When she was ready, she would. That was all. Nor was she allowed to complain about her husband. "It's better if he's perfect."

"He's not," said Elizabeth. "He's terminally shallow. He's..."

She would have gone on, but he stopped her. "Don't."

From time to time he announced they would be having children. On occasion he favoured all girls, more often a mixture. "At least three."

"I can't! No babies." She clutched at her stomach. No need to explain she spoke the literal truth. It was all too fantastic.

He even quoted poetry to her. "Of course, Yeats isn't perfect, but listen to this. 'Remember then...'" The sound of his voice ran all through her. He lifted his eyes to her face with an expression so full of love she felt herself sway. She almost loved him back then, as if by reflex, the way she bowed back to Mr. Chen. "'...how one man loved the pilgrim soul in you and loved the sorrows of your changing face...'"

"How do you know about my sorrows?" she asked startled.

"I know," Ted told her. But she turned away from him then.

She has been floating for several years now. The appeal of the absence of pain has thrived on the memory of pain. The death of the baby. The defection of Rodney. The months of sickness. These events have receded into the more distant and therefore bearable past. And lately Hong Kong, shimmering and unreal, has reinforced this idea, that she can somehow stay out of life. Married to Rodney, privy to the smaller pleasures, she believes she has made her bargain.

Ted's kiss, his hand on her head, were like blessings. She was not to worry. "It's okay," he said and helped her to button her dress. In time it would all come out right.

And this is how he is. Elizabeth can close her eyes any time and feel the warm bath of his confidence, his fingers climbing steadily up her back. He doesn't struggle over the moments. Things will go his way in the end. Such is his credo, his faith. In business he has made a good deal of success on this basis; his acquisitions have been swift, his decisions for the most part correct. The Chinese have told him they can feel his luck.

Elizabeth is standing in the street now, the last of the packages in her arms. Bored with climbing and carrying, she glances up to see if the maid has reappeared and instead sees Mr. Chen burst out of his own door. He is waving his arms high in the air, as though they are flagpoles. And he is screaming. The chauffeur leaps out of the Datsun and shouts something back. Mr. Chen screams again. He is not saying anything, just screaming. The chauffeur goes bounding up the stairs, taking them two at a time, zigzagging up. Mr. Chen starts down, stumbles, picks himself up. He and the chauffeur meet. Mr. Chen speaks, and the chauffeur continues on up and rushes into the house leaving the door wide open. Elizabeth's maid has appeared again at the top of their stairs. She starts down. Elizabeth watches her for a second and then, compelled by Mr. Chen's frenzy, crosses over to the foot of his stairway. He is plunging down the last steps, practically falling. Elizabeth stops, uncertain what is wrong. Because clearly something is. The man's face is distorted, his mouth wide and curved like a tragedy mask. All his teeth show. He flings himself at Elizabeth and clutches her arm.

"What is it? What is it?" she asks. Her packages fall into the street. He is saying something to her. His fingers hurt her arm. Above them she sees the chauffeur come out of the house. He leans over the railing and vomits. Beside her, more or less into her ear, Mr. Chen is saying something, repeating something. In Cantonese. The syllables are like bells ringing. Her maid has come up to them and peers at Elizabeth and then at Mr. Chen. She says something to him. For a second he ignores her, then turns and says something in return. As he speaks, her mouth drops. She shakes her head as if to say no, no. She turns and stares at Elizabeth. It is one of those moments between time. Get me out of this, thinks Elizabeth. Don't tell me!

"Dead," says the maid. She hesitates and then places her fingers and thumbs around her neck. She doesn't know the word for strangle, thinks Elizabeth.

There is a sound like a growl or a moan. Mr. Chen is making it through his nostrils which are distended and white.

"What?" says Elizabeth. "Who?" The chauffeur is coming down the stairs toward them. His eyes are wide and stunned. He wipes his chin with a handkerchief. Elizabeth thinks it's lucky he had one and, then, that none of this can be happening. She hears her own voice, far away, knife-thin. "Dead? Who's dead?"

The maid says something interrogative to Mr. Chen, who nods without ceasing his keening.

"The children too," says the maid in a voice like stones dropping. She blinks, then blinks again. Tears well out of her old, heavy-lidded eyes.

"Everyone's dead?" says Elizabeth to no one in particular. This *cannot* be happening. Mr. Chen has begun to sway, and she puts her arm around the small shoulders. A smell rises from his head. Vegetable oil frying, thinks Elizabeth. She will remember this and the rough wool of his suit against her fingertips... Not the children.

"Did you phone the police?" she says to the chauffeur. He stares at her. "Police," she says in Mandarin. Mr. Chen is still swaying in the curve of her arm. "Telephone." The chauffeur turns around and looks up at the house, then turns again and looks back at Elizabeth. He appears stymied. "My house," she tells him. He nods then and runs along the sidewalk and up her stairs, still wiping his mouth with the handkerchief.

That night there is a party. Elizabeth says she can't go. Rodney says this one is a must. Besides it will do her good. After all there is nothing she can do for the Chens. For Mr. Chen. Which is true. Hordes of relatives have arrived next door. The police are still there. The street is a mess of people. The whole Healthy and Happy Garden has been cordoned off. There will be no more crimes there. Not for the time being. And the party will give her something else to think about.

Elizabeth puts on a great deal of makeup and a silver-coloured dress. It is of heavy smooth silk, bare at the top with narrow straps. With her shining dress and hair and round, unfocused eyes she looks softer than usual, younger. Even Rodney, usually taciturn on such subjects, is moved to comment on this. "Nice," he tells her. He reaches out and touches her shoulder, as though he's making sure she's real. "Better take a sweater," he adds after a moment. "You know what the air conditioning is like in these places."

At the party she leans on the men's arms and laughs at everything they say. Wives are annoyed until word gets around and eventually she is accorded a measure of tolerance. She drinks champagne, at one point spilling a full glass, but the silver dress dries and the streaks barely show. After the cocktail party, she and Rodney and two other couples take a taxi to the Regent Hotel. This is in the nature of a treat and has required some discussion. The Regent Hotel is staggeringly expensive. It is also possibly the most elegant hotel in the world and certainly the most elegant that they have ever seen. Rolls Royces line up outside to take the hotel guests wherever they wish to go. Inside, the entrance lobby is all polished marble that gleams like clear ice. A wide alabaster staircase curves up and out of sight like a certain path to the angels. At the next level down, a long series of picture windows reveals the whole harbour and the illuminated gold and silver skyscrapers of Hong Kong rising out of the water and reaching up one behind the other and behind them the mountains rising still higher.

The hotel is indeed heavily air conditioned. Elizabeth shivers—she has left her sweater at the party—and one of the men gallantly rubs her arms. Rodney is doing the women in his urbane way, lighting a cigarette and indicating his office building with it. "Fabulous city," he says to the couple who are newcomers. "You'll go crazy shopping," he tells the women. "Everything in the world is for sale here."

They decide to eat in the grill downstairs. Everyone foreign in Hong Kong is forever sick of Chinese food even though it is Cantonese and the best in the world. Dinner will of course be expensive, but this is business promo. The two men are exporters. They will want to get money out of the country, sell goods in Canada, arrange deals. The Hong Kong stock exchange is kaput, one of the men tells Rodney. Rodney nods. He will be able to help them, his expression implies.

The waiter leads them to a table by the window. Another waiter places their napkins in their laps. This performance has always amused Elizabeth; tonight it makes her feel hysterical. She wants to ask if they will help her blow her nose.

"Yes, it was awful," she replies to one of the women who has solicitously asked about the events of the afternoon. And then gradually she becomes aware—she can hear her own voice going on and on with a description of the stairs and the three Chinese people and herself climbing and descending—she becomes aware that she feels nothing at all about what she is saying. It is like waking up dead. She sees these people, registers their nods, their little grimaces, but they are not really here. Or she is not really here. She rubs her arms. Tomorrow, of course, she will read about the deaths in the English-language paper. She will know how they died, the mother and the two little boys, will know who killed them perhaps. And then, surely, she will feel what any normal human being would feel.

Fingering the edges of her napkin, she sits up straighter in her chair. Across the harbour the skyscrapers appear to have receded; the sheet of water has darkened to a greenish bronze. The colour of storms. Somewhere near the bottom of her stomach, which is pressed against the tight waistband of the silver dress, the knowledge exists, the fear and the sorrow. She knows this. Yet the essence of her remains on the far shore, protected, she would say, by the rift inside her. Once more she sees her maid with hands around her own neck, the chauffeur wiping himself, Mr. Chen swaying in the street.

"Please," she says to the waiter who is pouring out the wine. "More." Rodney glances at her. "Right up," she instructs the waiter, who manages not to look either surprised or disdainful.

She lifts her brimming glass to the others, then drinks and raises the glass to them again, gazing over the rim into their eyes in the Chinese way. She looks from face to face as if trying to identify them. "Oh, yes," she says coming around to her husband. "You."

"Elizabeth," he says warningly.

They all have steaks, big juicy sirloins. Dead meat, thinks Elizabeth, giving hers a poke. She eats very little and continues to drink. During dessert, which is a fluffy, beige pie that tastes like a Brandy Alexander, she turns to the man on her right. "I plan to leave Rodney," she tells him by way of conversation.

"For Christ's sake, Elizabeth," says Rodney across the table. "Don't take it out on us." He is being patient, but he looks as if he knows what he'd like to say to her.

Taking his cue from Rodney, the man on her right decides to laugh indulgently. "Sure," he says. "Leave the son of a bitch." The women look taken aback, but the men all laugh. Then the women laugh too.

On the way back to Hong Lok Yuen, Rodney says nothing at first. Before their departure from the Regent Hotel, Elizabeth spent a quarter of an hour throwing up in the marble ladies' room, so perhaps he has put her behaviour down to an excess of wine. Finally, however, when they have broken through the traffic of downtown, he clears his throat. "I wish you wouldn't pull stuff like that," he tells her. "I mean that crap about leaving me. I mean I know you've had a hell of a shock and all that, but..." He shakes his head and then glances over at her. The headlights of an oncoming car flash over his high-bridged nose. She catches the glint of his eyes as he glances briefly in her direction. Then his features glide into shadow once again. Only the immutable line of his jaw remains visible as a faint, metallic gleam. Like a bronze casting, she thinks, cold to the touch. "Even though you don't mean it," he says. He has been in the process of changing lanes. Now he guns the car into the first of the upward curves.

"I don't know what I mean," she says.

He glances over at her again. "I hardly see why I'm to blame for a crime that happens next door," he says.

"You're not."

"Then what's the point of pulling something like that? I mean, if you were trying to make me look like a chump, that was as good a performance as any."

"Sorry," she says then. "I'm sorry." She can't remember really how she felt when she said those things in the Regent Hotel. The urge to say them has disappeared. It was the presence of near-strangers that prompted her, she thinks, the possibility that their reaction might tell her something she needed to know.

When she married Rodney she loved him, she is sure. She has thought a lot about this question, concluding finally that her emotions at that time were in the range of normal, her reasons for marrying him no more immature than the average. The two of them seemed right for each other. They were young, full of the usual expectations, ready to marry. They made a handsome couple. That was all.

When the baby died, the grief itself animated her, the pulse of pain through her body. The pulse of anger too. She remembers certain scenes. The flesh-coloured mask of Rodney's face hovering above her as she lay in the hospital bed. His words like lines from a poorly-written play. "Listen, these things happen. The thing is not to let it get you down." The face, his face, nodding at her. His voice descending. "We'll have another one. Don't take it so hard. Maybe next time it'll even be a boy." She remembers the heat of her rage, how it rose through her neck into her face, how his voice petered out...and later the fever, rising like another, further anger through her body. And she remembers the quiet winter afternoon—there had been no visitors that day; snow drifted against the window—and the voice of the doctor explaining that her adhesions were too extensive, she must never try another pregnancy.

"Not even any little girls," was what she said to Rodney that night, before she turned her head away and tried to weep.

For the breakdown, they gave her more drugs, and counselling, of course, and then a kind of group therapy. People in bathrobes sitting around on metal chairs, the arguing and crying, the ardent justifying of small cruelties, the silly arrogance of the group leader. This last experience—by its very ineptitude, she has decided since—prompted her first interest in clinical psychology.

When she got out of the hospital, Rodney was living with a trainee from his office. The girl came of unusual parentage, an Egyptian mother and a French father. She was small and dark-haired. Her perfume hung in the air. Elizabeth remembers the smell of it from the afternoon the girl made a pass at her in the back seat of a taxi, this after the three of them had met for a long lunch of the carefully civilized variety.

Oddly enough it was that incident, the incredible moment when the girl's hand crept up the back of her neck, insinuating itself like a thief into her hair, that decided Elizabeth. If things were this absurd, why not take Rodney back? What did it matter what he had said, what he had done, what he was or wasn't? He would be glad enough. She knew that. He thought of the two of them as a couple. He had said that. He was a conventional person. Probably, too, he wanted rescuing. He might even have been ashamed of himself.

Later, when she and Rodney were living together again, Elizabeth laughed about the pass, about the girl's determined seductiveness. But, in another way, she envied the girl her greed. Her lust for contact. Rodney said it was simple craziness, the girl was a screaming sex maniac. The scene in the taxi had been just more of the same for her. For him, on the other hand—and he had, he said, come to understand this—for him the affair had been a kind of reassurance, an interlude in which to get used to the idea of no children, to make his adjustment so to speak, to get, moreover, through the period of Elizabeth's breakdown, her departure from reality. She ought to understand it had been hard for him too.

The car has committed itself to the last and steepest climb, the hairpin curve up to the very brink of the Healthy and Happy Garden. Suddenly weary, Elizabeth leans her head against the window. Her hair slides across her cheek. She feels its caress like the whisper of someone lost, herself perhaps, or the baby, or the little boys. She thinks of the persistent flame that was the smaller one's body, of his spiky hair and spindly arms. She never touched her own baby. The baby died, tiny and wrinkled, in the incubator. Elizabeth never touched her.

At home, despite her fatigue, she moves restlessly about the house, striding into rooms as if something awaits her there, drifting out again moments later. Rodney gets up to complain that she is keeping him awake and states once again the incontrovertible fact that there is nothing in the world that she can do.

"I know that," she says.

"You're making it worse," he tells her. "You won't let things go."

"I'm not making it worse," says Elizabeth. "It happened. A horrible, horrible thing."

He makes a gesture of irritation and retreats to the bedroom. Ten minutes later he is back.

"Look," he says to Elizabeth. "Look, if it really bothers you, we'll move. For these last months. The company can handle it." He glances at her to see if she is responding. "Of course, an arrangement like this...it'll take a week or two to implement it."

"To implement it?" Elizabeth repeats.

He looks sharply at her, but she makes no sign. "You know what I mean," he says. "The apartment's not just sitting there empty. Not with the rent the company's carrying on it."

On paper, Elizabeth is thinking, Rodney still looks good. He really does. Even his height seems an attribute especially directed at her. "It doesn't matter," she says suddenly.

"You're sure?" he asks. She sees the relief smoothing the crease between his eyebrows. Probably he can't help coming in at the level he does. She ought to remember that. Probably it's the way he's put together. "I mean," he is saying, "I don't mind. I'll just tell them." He bends to kiss the top of her head.

"It doesn't matter," she says again and begins to shake her head. "Go to sleep. It wouldn't make any difference if we moved. Dead is dead."

"True," he says agreeably. He has already turned on his heel. A moment later the bedroom door clicks shut.

Feelings are the truest means of knowing. Ted has said this to her many times, that he trusts his feelings. They are the source of his hunches, the secret of his famous, so-called good luck.

In the dimness she smells the incense she bought last week with him in Kowloon. Only one stick of it has been burned, but the faint cinnamon aroma lingers. Finally just before she gives up and goes to bed, she decides to say a prayer for Mr. Chen and his family. Kneeling beside the sofa with her forehead bowed to touch the glass top of the coffee table, she prays to an unknown Chinese god. Help them.

Help me, she thinks of adding. But the enormity of their tragedy is too great to intrude upon. Instead she tiptoes across the carpeted hallway to turn off the lights and feels suddenly in her bare feet and long nightgown, with her prayers said and unsaid, like the child she has never had.

Though they have spoken on the telephone several times, it is three days before she sees Ted again. They meet for lunch in a restaurant behind the Wing Kowloon Theatre. The ceiling of this restaurant is arched, the interior space marked off by screens, some of these gleaming black, some a milky green inlaid with mother-of-pearl. The black ones give back reflections and, sometimes, reflections of reflections, so that it is impossible to tell which surfaces are real and which will alter or even vanish as she approaches. Twice, crossing the room, she catches sight of herself, taller than everyone else in the restaurant, her hair like a shaft of light moving across the flat panel. These fleeting views make her feel safe, as though she has the choice of disappearing at anytime. The owner of the restaurant is a friend of Ted's. He has just bought the place and, part way through the meal, comes over to sit with them. Ted introduces him as C. K. Ng. C. K. comes from Singapore. His family has lived there since '48. "Overseas Chinese," he says, going on to explain that recently the family has bought a hotel here in Hong Kong. Prices of such real estate have dropped drastically since the Thatcher visit, but his family is confident for the longer run. His older brother is managing the hotel. The restaurant is C. K.'s baby. At the end of lunch, he summons a waiter and speaks to him in a language Elizabeth doesn't recognize. Glasses and a green, lantern-shaped bottle are brought to the table. "From San Francisco," C. K. tells them. He unscrews the top, sniffs at the bottle, and then pours out three glassfuls. "My mother brought it in last week." Elizabeth sips at hers. The flavour is fruity, but she can't decide what it is.

"Melon," says C. K. when they have failed to guess. He leans back in his chair and laughs. "My mother's crazy about sweet liqueurs, especially bright-coloured ones. She's always bringing back some crazy drink for the restaurant."

C. K. doesn't look to Elizabeth like the usual Chinese businessman. That is, he is not short and round with glued-down hair. Instead he is very slim. Even his face is narrow, and his black hair flops over his eyes when he laughs. He has to brush it back each time with his thin fingers. "What part of the States are you from?" he asks Elizabeth.

She shakes her head. "Canada. Montreal."

"Ah," says C. K. nodding. "McGill. I have two cousins there. One in engineering, one at medical school. "

"McGill's where I'm doing my degree," she says. "Or, rather, where I was doing it."

C. K. nods again. He himself, he says, went to Stanford.

"Overseas Chinese," says Ted. "Anywhere you can think of, C. K.'s been. Or he's got a cousin studying there."

C. K. grins. Then he pushes back his chair and gets to his feet. "Listen, I've got to speak to those guys over there before they leave." He indicates with his head a corner table surrounded by men in dark suits and once more brushes the hair from his face. "You call me later, Ted, say about five. I have news coming from Taipei." Ted nods, and C. K. turns to Elizabeth. "I like doing business with this guy. Very lucky."

"That's Ted," says Elizabeth.

C. K. smiles at Elizabeth. "You come to my restaurant again, okay? You're lucky too." He glances at Ted. "You call me this afternoon, okay?"

"Right," says Ted. He and C. K. shake hands.

The restaurant is emptying out now. The businessmen are leaving in groups of two and three, all bowing, all seemingly talking at once. Ted places his hand over Elizabeth's. "You all right?"

For a moment she is actually able to imagine what it would be like to lay her head on his hand and weep, to tell him that she has been wondering where and in what sort of place her baby exists. She draws in a breath, then shakes her head. "Don't worry about me," she says. "It doesn't bother me. It doesn't matter."

Behind his glasses Ted's eyes open wide. "Of course it matters."

"I mean...that it happened next door doesn't matter. I didn't know them really."

"Sure, you knew them. Kids..." He looks sad, as if he too remembers standing in the street, the willow wand arm, the hair like black flames. "You know," he says, "most people, when evil surfaces, they're shocked. They can't believe what's out there. But you're not surprised. Some day, you must tell me why."

For another moment he holds her hand in both of his. Then he places the hand, her hand, down on the table cloth as if he is giving it back to her. "Come on," he says. "We'll get the bill and take a walk. I have an hour or so, and there's a little jade cat in Wu Ling's window that you have to see." Obediently she unhooks her purse from the chair back. Maybe, she is thinking, maybe the mother of the little boys will watch over the baby now, sing her something Chinese when she cries. Ted pushes his chair back and gets up. Across the room C. K. Ng flashes a smile at them. His sheaf of black hair flops forward as he bows.

During their walk Ted again holds her hand. In spite of the heat, she is glad to feel the warmth against her skin. After a moment she glances sideways at his face. Sweat glistens along his hairline. She thinks of rubbing it away but doesn't.

Just before C. K. joined them at the restaurant, Ted was talking about an apartment he wanted to buy on Hong Kong Island. "Not hung up there on the cliffs like a lot of them...three walls and a view. This is a place we could live in." C. K. came over to the table before Ted got any further. At the time, she welcomed being let off the hook. Now, though, she should probably bring up the subject again, tell Ted once and for all that she is incapable of making such a move. They dodge around a crowd of teenagers in the middle of the sidewalk, and she opens her mouth to speak. But the reasons she ought to give him escape her.

Ted looks over at her now. "This jade cat we're going to see," he says. "It's like you, shiny but the light doesn't go through it." She stares back at him, thinking of the cool green of jade, how glassy it is and how hard. "You're looking lost," he adds. "Wu Ling's is around this next corner."

"It's nice you know everything," she says and catches the edge of his smile before, involuntarily, she glances up at the next cluster of signs, seeking among them the characters she can decipher.

They are all packed, she and Rodney. The door is locked. These suitcases cluttering the road are all that remain of their whole Hong Kong life. In her purse Elizabeth carries the little jade cat. It is her only true memento of the year. She has never gone on the shopping spree as everyone told her she must. Toward the end, Rodney pressed her to buy a few souvenirs—why not, the price would certainly have been right—but she refused. Twice she has told him she wants a divorce...both times, it must be admitted, at parties, so he doesn't really believe her. She has been strange anyway since the murders. He has told her this, and she knows it's true. Especially when she drinks. It's part of a reaction to the tragedy, no doubt, although sometimes she thinks it is Hong Kong altogether. The absence of a common language, the excessive, exotic atmosphere, everything so tall and grand or crowded and teeming. A city out of her ken, and growing more so. Sometimes she is convinced she can't see the shore of Hong Kong Island any more, as though the city has slipped away. Although more likely it is simply that it cannot now be for her what she meant it to be. Yet, in another way, it suits her better for the enigma it has become. A place where she cannot possibly fathom reasons. A place where beauty has been able to take the place of happiness.

At the end of the street, just before the taxi sweeps them around the bend, away from the Healthy and Happy Garden forever, she turns and looks back. The two houses, theirs and the Chens', lean toward one another, as if they are straining to touch, to offer one another comfort. Then, abruptly, they flip away. The taxi has plunged into the hairpin turn. Elizabeth's brake foot stamps the floor. The taxi picks up speed, then slows again as its tires squeal into the next curve. Rodney gives her a distrustful glance but says nothing.

Curve by curve and squeal by squeal they descend the mountainside until they arrive at the main road and are swallowed up by the traffic. Now, as if to celebrate this triumph, the driver snaps on the radio. At the first syllables of the announcer's voice, Elizabeth sits forward again, hoping, as she always does, to catch a few words from the program. But it's no good. She still doesn't know enough to make sense of the announcements. Beside her, erect and responsible looking as he watches over the driver's shoulder, Rodney, too, seems foreign. She could almost say, as he turns to glance at her now, that his features match none in her memory.

"What?" she says after a moment. He has been speaking.

"Your ticket," he says with some exasperation. "Here." He hands her the travel agency folder. "In case we get separated. You have your passport?"

She stares at him. "Of course."

"Well," he says defensively, "You're very forgetful lately."

Without replying she pushes the folder into her purse. She could tell him about the rift inside her, that it may always be there, that it keeps her apart from the sorrow. But there would be no point; he wouldn't get it.

At the end of Nathan Road, the rows of red taxis have jammed together more tightly than usual, if that is possible. The light turns green, then red, then green again without their progressing more than half a block. The driver turns off the radio as if he may then be able to concentrate more effectively on getting them out of this mess. Beside her Rodney's lips have compressed into a white line. But, in fact, plenty of time remains. She glances at her watch. Yes. They will certainly make the flight. Rodney has allowed for Kowloon traffic.

She imagines the airport, their suitcases being trundled across the sidewalk, the crowds and the counters filled with blue and white Chinese vases, scrolls and fans and little embroidered purses. She thinks about standing in the middle of the floor there and staring up at the great black sign that lists outgoing flights. It is the kind of thing she and Ted could do. Chanting the names back and forth to each other. Dakar, Singapore, Bangkok, Bombay, Taipei, Tokyo.

When they said goodbye, Ted cried. The tears ran into the creases of his cheeks while Elizabeth stood transfixed. The end of his nose and the skin around his mouth turned a pitiful, childish pink. His heart was broken. He actually said that. "My heart is broken." But then he put his hands around her shoulders as though he still could shore her up.

"It isn't right," he told her, as though he and she, Ted and Elizabeth, were a decree of fate. She faced him in a sort of trance. I can't make the jump, she thought of saying. Help me. But the words stayed locked inside her like the enforced silence of a dream.

And yet there is something of him alive in her—the rough shape of his head beneath her hands, the exuberance of his particular faith, a faith which may now be broken—enough so that several times then and in the next few days, she has thought of going back to him, of putting her arms around him and saying that she has changed her mind, that she will stay. Benevolently she has pictured his happiness, the joy spreading over his plain and pleasant face. Then why hasn't she let it happen? Because she is afraid? Because his wish that she love him is not enough to make it happen? Because there is some other issue at stake?

Now, suddenly, she thinks there was something she meant to tell him. Twice she has dreamed about the Chens. Though she knows that the case will probably never be solved—everyone says it was an underworld matter—though she tells herself the children and their mother are dead forever, still a strange, unbidden thought is loose in her mind. She has dreamed of the return of Mrs. Chen and the two children, children whose names she doesn't know, whose faces she is beginning to forget. In her dream they are brought back by Ted. There has been a miracle, he explains to Elizabeth. Together they climb the stairs and deliver the children and their mother to the welcoming arms of Mr. Chen.

Ahead of them the light turns green again, and tears begin to slide down Elizabeth's face. The sensation shocks her. Tears? The warm salty wash of them. She can taste it on her lips. The taxi still hasn't moved.

Rodney is gazing at her with shocked eyes. "You never cry," he says. "What's the matter? There's enough time. We'll make it."

"I'm crying for Mr. Chen," she says, "and Mrs. Chen and the little boys."

Rodney shakes his head. Then he tries to hand her his handkerchief. "Here, come on," he says. "You're going to snap again if you're not careful." She takes the handkerchief. Their taxi begins to inch forward. She looks up and sees that they are almost to the intersection. The exit onto the highway is nearly in sight. They will be there in no time now. No time. Without warning, panic floods her. She looks around, stares for a second at Rodney's intent profile. It's not just the death of the baby, this rift inside her. It's the decay that spreads in the absence of life. She is disappearing from the inside out. Her stomach tightens. Quick. This moment, this red light, may be her last chance.

She ignores a sensible, Rodney-like voice within her which says that she is being a trifle dramatic. Instead she drops the handkerchief and reaches into her purse. Her fingers brush the hard paper edge of the ticket folder. "Here," she says pulling it out of her bag. "Here." She hands the folder to Rodney, who is so astonished he takes it. His mouth opens, but she holds up one finger, as though he can be silenced in this way. "Leave my bags at the airport," she tells him and sees that the light has turned green once again. "No, don't." She opens the car door and thrusts her foot out onto the pavement.

"What in hell...?" Rodney begins.

"Have the driver deliver them to someone's flat," she interrupts. "I can call around."

By now she has climbed out and is standing in the street and leaning back into the taxi. After the car's frigid air conditioning, the outdoor heat surrounds her like a blanket. Behind the taxi, horns begin to honk. "Elizabeth, for Christ's sake!" shouts Rodney. "Get in the fucking taxi!"

"I can't," she tells him. "I'm sorry."

"Are you out of your mind?" he shouts. "Why do you do these things? We don't have that much time." He looks ready to cry himself. "I can't just leave you here."

"I'm leaving *you* here, Rodney." She takes a backward step, out of his reach. "I'm sorry, I didn't know." She nods at him and then adds soothingly, "Go on. You don't want to miss the plane." She shuts the door and, slipping between the cars in the next lane, reaches the sidewalk. Then she swings off in the opposite direction, shouldering her purse and snaking between the people, breathing in the hothouse air as though this is her first moment on earth. Her long strides cover the distance quickly, but not until the end of the second block does she risk looking back. There is no sign of Rodney. She is sure she would see him above the throng.

Perhaps the taxi is already out of sight. For once Rodney is on the highway, won't he proceed to the airport? And once at the airport, ticket in hand, won't he be carried on by the precision and completeness of his various arrangements? Won't he board the plane and be gone? Maybe. She'll find out soon enough.

It will not of course be the settling of everything if he does leave, but at least there will be nothing more to say. She hurries through the next intersection with the sense that she is crossing some final divide. Which of her friends will she go to? Not someone connected with the company. Someone at the university then? Or Ted? No, not Ted. All this has nothing to do with lovers.

It is at the next corner, when she sees a poster for the Wing Kowloon Theatre, that she thinks of C. K. Ng's restaurant, of his airy invitation that she come by any time. She conjures up his narrow face and body, his merry smile. The theatre is around the corner, the restaurant therefore no more than a couple of blocks' walk. She will sweep, like the tall pale foreigner she is, into the Chinese world, into C. K. Ng's restaurant, that is. She can make phone calls from there, count her money, organize her thoughts; it's the perfect resting spot. She can even take tea there, and a glass of C. K. Ng's mother's melon liqueur. They will let her in, let her do all this, and they will not care whether she has left her husband, why she is there, why she is anywhere at all.

She pushes the hair back from her cheeks and tries to see her reflection in the next plate glass window. For an instant she catches the streak of long pale hair, the shape of her fast-moving body. Then the image, superimposed on a bolt of cloth, is gone. Like the image of a hoped-for child, here and then gone. A matter of luck. Send for the Fung Shui man...the best anyone can do...and the rest belongs to luck.

The idea of luck makes her think again of Ted. Ted, whom she hardly knows. Ted, who will have to be told she cannot bear children. Perhaps that truth alone will finish him. Or perhaps it won't finish him, and the sorrow, resurrected, will be passed on. Sorrow. She says this word in her mind, feeling it over, thinking of her younger self and again of Mr. Chen and the death of children. So sad. But all the same it is exhilaration that fills her now. Above her head the forest of signs flashes. Horns honk. Lighter than air, strong as the earth, she flies along the crowded street staring into window after window, not slackening her pace, no longer bothering to seek her reflection in the glass. The luxuries of Hong Kong—a million gold chains and watches, pens and jewelry, pearls in folds of silk and velvet, topaz, ebony, ivory, amethysts and jade, a veritable garden crystallized out of time and the earth itself—all this stares back at her from the shop windows. And it is all so beautiful.

RABBITS

"All that cognac," Janey says. "And Jacques making those geriatric runs at the girls from your office..." She has to pitch her voice high in order to be heard over the rattle of the car heater. So far its efforts haven't counted for much. The air around her ankles has stayed chilly. In the back seat, the children are still wearing their mittens and tuques.

Karl shrugs. "It was a party." Another blast of wind shakes the little Chevrolet; Janey can see the skin around his fingernails whiten.

"My head hurts," she says for perhaps the third time. "Right where cognac always gets me..." She follows this with a noisy sigh. He says nothing, and after a moment she speaks again, this time in the new, hard voice she is practicing. "I told Eleanor we had a lot in common...she and I, I mean."

"Jesus," he says without vehemence. "That needling bitch?"

"I think I meant that you and Jacques were a lot alike." Jacques is Karl's boss. He is also a womanizer of note.

Karl's head swivels a couple of inches. His eyes that seem always to have the light of the sky in them swing in her direction. "That's another charming idea," he says. She draws in a sharp breath, and then she hesitates.

She, after all, is the one who believes in family outings. This morning she trailed from room to room sipping coffee and picking up toys—clumps of Lego mostly and Peter's tiny ubiquitous racing cars (the apartment gets easily cluttered)—while she sold the idea of a ride. Peter was sucked in by the bridge and the riverside park, but it was Sally Jane, hopping around over the prospect of rapids, who got Karl to agree.

"Were you smoking stuff too?" she asks him now, making her voice conciliatory. "I saw that dealer friend of theirs over in the corner."

He nods. "It feels like I've been driving down this road forever."

"Who was that black-haired girl? She was smoking too. The one who hung around you all night and did that dance with the lamp?"

His head doesn't move. "She's one of Jacques's new assistants."

"Well, she certainly was having a good time with you..."

"Come on," says Karl. "Lay off, will you. She's like that...a party is just a party."

This silences her. He has been telling her the same thing for years, that things don't matter as much as she thinks, that people don't mean what they say...that what she, Janey, calls her instinct is merely a habit of jumping to conclusions. "A party is just a party." The sentence bubbles in her mind. We met at a party, she thinks of saying...but doesn't. Instead she turns and glances out her window.

In the blowing grass along the highway, in the brown fields that stretch to the horizon...no hint of summer green, nothing of softness. All gone, she thinks, searching the landscape, noting the shabby farmhouses, the patches of trees few and far between, sheltering nothing. Typical Sunday in November.

The party—not last night's but the long ago one where they met—was the kind people gave in those days. With an amorphous guest list and the usual offerings...beer and chips and a sticky, powerful punch served in paper cups, cigarettes and records, pillows on the floor, possibly someone with a guitar and a few joints...

Janey no longer remembers what she was wearing. Something black maybe, or a strong blue that suited her flushed skin and brown eyes. What she does remember is Karl's air of being above it all and then, later as he crossed the room toward her, his ice-coloured eyes, startling beneath straight, dark eyebrows. Quite simply, he was the most attractive man at the party. For no better reason she chose him that night.

Afterward, of course, she found other things to admire in him; she fell in love with him. And on the first weekend of May that year, she took him up to her parents' place in the Laurentians. A prim collar of ice still edged the lake, but the willows along the shore had sprouted a gauzy veil of green, and even from the car window the woods smelled fertile with last fall's decomposing leaves.

Almost as soon as they arrived, she took him out for a walk. They followed the path along the lake, stopping occasionally to test the shoreline ice, and then cut back across an unplowed field. By the end of the walk, shadows were mushrooming among the trees. He took her arm and pointed toward the ridge of granite that rose from the woods behind the house, the crest still lit like the jagged edge of a ruin. "The sun hasn't set up there," he said.

She stared around uneasily. "It's getting sort of dark..."

"Come on," he said. "There's plenty of time."

And, of course, he was right. On the summit they stood glazed in sunlight once again. Below them, like an offering, lay the big half-timbered house and, beyond it, a stretch of winter-blackened woods sloping off toward the lake. She let her glance slide around to Karl's face and saw, to her surprise, that the rather soldierly mien which so often stiffened his expression had fled. Perhaps it was only the bronze light, but it seemed that pleasure lay soft and glowing on his features. He looked revealed. He caught her glance, and the hand that had been resting lightly on the back of her neck tightened. For a moment she thought he was going to bend and kiss her. But his face came no nearer. Instead he nodded, as if he were agreeing with something she'd said or done.

"It's a great place." His voice came out thick, and he had to clear his throat. "I'd love a place like this...land...a real mansion... You must love coming back here."

She stared at him and then slowly, compelled by something in his face, nodded back. Her mouth remained poised for the kiss. For a long time she could feel the imprint where it should have settled on her lips, and the disappointment made a tiny, empty place inside her. Yet the words were for him so personal that in another way she was touched...and surprised too. Wasn't he showing himself to her really, by exposing a wish, by admitting something that he longed for?

"It was my grandparents' place. My father's always complaining how the upkeep's terrific."

Karl turned to smile at her. "The structure looks pretty sound," he said encouragingly. "A little weathered..."

She interrupted his analysis of the roof's condition by tugging on his arm. "I meant to tell you about my father, actually. Sometimes he's kind of rough on people. I meant to warn you. And my mother cries at the drop of a hat."

Karl reached around her waist and pulled her back against him. "You worry too much," he said into her ear. "Don't worry."

"Cold," she protested as his hand slid up under her jacket.

When she opened her eyes a few moments later, the sun had left them once again, this time for good, and the woods off in the distance had fused into a monolith of darkness. Against it the house loomed, man-made and comforting, the big oblong windows of the kitchen faintly aglow.

"So relax about your father," he was telling her. "I'll survive him. People don't bother me..." With his free hand he pointed over her shoulder toward the furthest section of the house. His leather sleeve brushed her cheek. The quality of his voice remained solemn. "That wing," he said. "It does look like it needs work. Look. You can see it's out of kilter...the foundation must have shifted."

She tipped back her head to look at him. He was staring over her head toward the house. "Your hand's pretty warm now," she told him. Then she reached up and cupped the side of his face with her hand.

She believes she can still remember that single touch. Among the thousands that have followed it. She can still feel, she is sure, the twin ridges of jawline and cheekbone. From that particular twilit moment she can pull it all back, even wince again at the sudden scratch of stubbled skin against her palm.

She recalls, almost as well, the next evening...her father drinking pre-dinner scotches from a shot glass, rattling the pages of the newspaper, occasionally looking up to command their attention with some caustic remark about a politician.

Her mother absorbed these conversational jabs with little nods and placating sounds. Her freckled hands meanwhile lept and weaved like frenetic birds above the pile of knitting in her lap...their rhythm known perfectly, subliminally, to everyone in the room except Karl. Minute by minute the bulky green folds acquired new dimension.

At the other end of the room, the fire was in danger of breaking up. Embers flared, then tumbled to tiny deaths on the flagstone hearth. Her father rose to get a log from the woodbasket. He tossed this onto the glowing remnants, then for some moments stood prodding the burning ends of wood until he had coaxed a flame around the new log. When he returned to his chair, his face bore a look of satisfaction, as though he had proved some heavily contested point. Ever alert for signals, Janey saw this look and allowed herself to relax. As he sat down, she turned to ask her mother a question.

"Non-stop handouts!" The sudden roar made them all jump. Janey's drink sloshed over her hand. Her father was leaning forward in his big armchair. She stared at him for a second, then realized his glare was focused on the coffee table. Of course! Her university grant application. Not three feet from him...oh, the carelessness of it. For the war cry about "hand-outs" was one she knew well. It categorized offenses related to the dwindling of his capital, a shrinkage which proceeded directly from one or another manifestation of the welfare state. That was the thesis.

Her father, loose now, ranted on—Canada had evidently done no right for decades—until he reached the stage of repeatedly smacking the coffee table with his newspaper. As if he were slapping each of them. At this point two things happened. Her mother began to cry into the bulky green sweater. And Karl stood up. He rose in a single, athletic motion, accompanied but seemingly untouched by the mingled sounds of weeping and shouting. His gaze swung around to rest on the congested features of her father. Janey watched, stiff with embarrassment. Karl looked as if he were observing a demented zoo animal. Her father was now in the act of crushing the front section of the paper. "No hypocrite on God's earth like a rich socialist!" he roared, glaring from one to the other of them as if they had each in turn argued otherwise. "This country's got herself a pantywaist prime minister who can't... Where are you going, young man?" Still glaring, he paused for breath.

Karl's cool voice filled the sudden space. "I'm going for a walk. I'll be back for dinner." This latter statement he addressed exclusively to her green-shrouded mother.

From her misery Janey watched him turn and cross the room. Not until he was almost in front of her own chair, did she realize he wasn't simply leaving the room. His eyes flickered once as he gazed down at her—no further expression crossed his dark-browed face—and then he held out his hand. She stared for a second at the outstretched fingers.

"You're coming?" He spoke softly, but to Janey the words rang like a declaration. Without further thought she was on her feet.

All down the darkening path to the lake, she felt magically, dazzlingly female. Rescued. He had rescued her. Her whole body felt warm. They picked their way over the rocks and slid on their heels down the packed wet leaves, and all the time she was sure that her life would not be the same again. In that terrible, wonderful moment—when he held out his hand to her, and she reached up and took it, and the crying and shouting were reduced to background static—she had felt the change. Something of herself had fused with him. She wanted to tell him this but could think of no words that could encircle and deliver whole such a glorious feeling. Ahead of them a rabbit skittered across the path. Without speaking she squeezed Karl's arm. A faint friendly rustle sounded from the woods, then nothing but silence.

At the water's edge they drew together. Her body sighed and bent into his. Over his shoulder, before she closed her eyes, she saw the light gleam gently off the surface of the lake. It was that twilight hour of evening, the same hour as yesterday's moment of truth up on the bluff. And now, with the last vestige of observational power left in her, she recognized the moment, this moment, as the most perfect of her existence...more perfect than any time in the past...more perfect, as it came to happen, than the hour she spent in his bed that night...more perfect, she would say now, than any moment since.

She glances at him now, notes the shadow around his finely carved nostril, the hollow engraved in his cheek. "I talked to that man Rowan for a while," she says casually. "Sort of pompous..."

"Oh, he's okay. Just the kind of guy who goes after things." Karl's voice, since he doesn't look at her, sounds disconnected, as if he's dropping the words somewhere between them.

"We should have a party," she announces. "We've been to Eleanor and Jacques's a million times."

"Sure," says Karl. "Why not?"

"I want a hot dog."

Janey glances around. Peter is regarding her with dispirited eyes. "We'll have a snack after we see the rapids," she assures him.

"See rabids," murmurs Sally Jane. She looks nearly asleep.

"Rapids, love," says Janey. "We'll be there soon." She turns back to Karl. "A party with some of your office people, some of the ones I've met at Eleanor and Jacques's, the black-haired girl, for instance..." She sees his lips part, catches the slight lowering of his eyelids.

"Francine?" he says now. "Sure, she's good fun." His voice is noncommittal.

"And Rowan maybe..."

"Why not?" Karl says again. He gives her a distracted glance. His hands, both of them, remain on the wheel guarding against the vagaries of the wind. His hair—and she decides this vengefully—his hair is less bright than it used to be. Duller. Flatter. But his profile still cuts the grey sky and the frame of the window as precisely as ever. What has changed is that it no longer seems part of him. It simply is.

Occasionally Janey studies Peter and Sally Jane to see if he has bequeathed this particular look to either of them. Such an inheritance for her children would make the betrayals less bitter.

Karl's affair lasted a little over a year. Until the week Sally Jane took her first step, to be exact. Janey thinks the affair was intense, though Karl has never admitted this. Nor has he ever named the woman. Janey is pretty sure she was one of his customers, the young widow of a wealthy and much older man. But Karl has never said.

"It had nothing to do with you," was as far as he got.

"That's fine then," Janey said. "That makes me feel just fine." They were standing in the bedroom. She stared down at the perfume bottle on her dresser—he had given it to her at Christmas—and then back at him. He was gazing out the window, the one that faced directly across the lane into the brick wall of another apartment building. A flush had risen up his neck into his cheeks; the cords of his neck stood out. His features looked not so much defiant as temporarily paralyzed. At that moment Peter wandered into the room, and Karl, hearing his step, whirled and grabbed him up as though the floor were a dangerous place.

"I'm sorry," he said then, staring at her over Peter's shoulder, and she saw that he had tears in his eyes.

Later on, as if to affirm where his heart lay, he began to bring home presents for the children. A series of racing cars for Peter. A jack-in-the-box and a giant yellow bunny for Sally Jane. The bunny, which has huge floppy ears, is as large as Sally Jane is now. She drags it around, bossing and scolding it, and at night she insists it sit at the foot of her bed. (It's too large to put under the covers with her.)

Around the same time as the presents, Janey grew her hair long. She lost ten pounds and took to wearing eye makeup and flirting heavily at parties. Now, no matter how late and loud the party, she never wants to go home. It's as if, after dark, after the children are in bed, and especially after she has had a couple of drinks, a frenetic, single self reasserts its existence. Karl's affair happened less than two years ago; yet already she can hardly remember how she used to be.

Other things have happened since then as well. Three times Janey's mother has called to announce that her father is dying. He has not died, but a series of minor strokes has destroyed some of his memory and a good deal of his hearing. He no longer flies into rages. And while Janey certainly doesn't miss his dragon performances—who could?—his silence seems even worse...as if he is being tortured in some soundless way.

Karl has observed that the old house in the Laurentians may become too much for Janey's mother. They should consider buying it if they can dig up enough cash. His voice becomes animated as he lists repairs and improvements that might be worked on its aging frame.

"Bloody freezing," says Karl now. Sally Jane clings to his jacket as he sets her down. The wind is lashing the long brown grass of the park. It shakes the bushes—no more now than bunches of dried sticks—until they chatter.

"It's too late in the year," Janey admits. She clutches the flaps of her coat, then takes Peter's hand and hurries him on through the bushes. Directly ahead, they can see for the first time how fast the river is moving. Little waves writhe between the smooth-running ridges of water. Streaks of foam mark the actual stones.

"Imagine the Indians trying to get through all that in their canoes," she says to Peter.

"Are the Indians gone?" he asks. He tilts his head back to look up at her, and she sees that his tuque has slipped to his eyebrows. It's the new red one, slightly too large, that Karl brought home for him from a Canadiens' game.

"Here, love," she says reaching down to him. "How can you see anything?"

"Are they?" he insists as she adjusts the ribbed band.

"The Indians gone? Mostly. And the ones who're left have changed." We should have come a month ago, she is thinking, back when the grass was still fresh and leaves shuffled and whispered in the trees... She is still recalling to herself how the park would have been when she hears Karl's shout. Sally Jane's little body comes flying past, and a second later Karl too is past them.

Janey's scream disintegrates in the wind. She sees the forward curve of Karl's back, the reach of his arm as he catches up with the runaway. Then his hand closes on the little shoulder; Sally Jane's body is lifted almost off its racing feet.

Janey's heart is thudding so hard she can barely hear her own words. She looks down at Peter. "Don't you ever do that!" Peter shakes his head importantly.

"She's crazy," he says a moment later as they come up beside Karl and the still struggling Sally Jane.

"...Never again, honey. You hear me?" Karl has bent down and is speaking directly into Sally Jane's ear. Still she strains against his grasp, oblivious to warnings.

As Karl stands up now, his eyes meet Janey's. "Christ!" he says, "What's got into her?" The wind slices between them as he speaks, and for an instant she feels the old wish to hold his gaze.

But even as she opens her mouth to say something, his eyes slide away from hers. He glances toward the moving water and shrugs. What can we do, says this shrug, except what we have already done?

"Is this the park?" Peter tugs complainingly on her hand, and she lets her eyes drop to his affronted gaze. His tuque has descended to his eyebrows once again.

"Yes," she says. "Yes, love, it is the park. But it's colder than we thought, isn't it?"

He nods, and the four of them move forward to the river edge. Still held by Karl, Sally Jane leans out over the water. She stares intently into the flashing waves. There is no question that if he were not clutching her arm, she would fall directly into the water.

No question, either, that the little body believes it could fly if only the big hand would let it free. Janey squats down and slides an arm around her child. She spreads her hand over the convex midriff. "Listen, love," she says, speaking into the flimsy child's hair that blows across her face. "You can see. Really." With her free hand she points toward the foam. "The rapids come from stones that are just underneath the water. You can tell where they are by the little white waves. See the little white waves?"

Sally Jane nods. Then she twists around and glances up at Karl. "Daddy?" she says. Janey can barely discern the thread of her voice. "Daddy get 'em?"

Karl bends over her. "Daddy can't get them," he says shaking his head. "The rapids aren't something you can have. They stay in the water." He straightens up. "You've got her?" he says to Janey. She nods, and he lets go Sally Jane's arm.

Janey blinks. The cold is bringing tears to her eyes. Here at the very brink, the wind comes straight off the river, stripping the heat from their faces, slashing against their bare necks. They won't last long here. "Ugh," she says now. "Horrid wind."

Sally Jane looks back at her for a second. "Horrid wind," she repeats and then, her face full of hope, "Where the rabids?"

"Rapids, love. They're right there," Janey assures her. "Come on. It's cold. Let's go." As she pulls the child back from the grassy edge and stands up beside Karl, she is thinking of the coming of winter, the snow and the dark frigid mornings, the short days. How she will be cold all the time.

On the way home Janey hands out the cookies and cans of juice she has brought with them. "For Christ's sake," says Karl as she pops open the cans for the children. "We'll be home in half an hour. That stuff makes a hell of a mess." He dislikes mess. Besides, he's probably still feeling lousy. Janey's hand hesitates. Of course, he's right. The car seats will get even stickier. Crumbs will work their way into the cracks in the vinyl. Still...why shouldn't she do it her way? Rowan tells her she is spontaneous, that he enjoys that quality in her.

Handing back the cans of juice, she glances at Karl. But he is no longer paying attention. They are passing a row of elaborate old river houses, estates that once belonged to Montreal's rich and may still do so. Karl keeps glancing to his left. It's as if his eyes are sweeping up each precisely curved driveway, assessing the value and substance of each house. He nods now as if he's agreeing with himself. "If I get that wholesale marketing account and you go back to teaching next year, we could think about buying an old house." His glance swings around to her, then back again toward the river. The house they are passing is an old Tudor-style mansion, half-timbered like her parents' place. "Ask your mother, and your father, what they think."

"They're going to sell the house." Her voice cuts through the air between them...the new hard voice. "They're selling it to my cousin...the one who lives in Europe. He wants a place to come to in the summers. My mother wants to keep it in the family..."

There is a slight, rigid movement in the muscles at the corners of his mouth and in the cords of his neck. "She would have told us," he says.

"She did...I mean, she told me. Last weekend. She asked me what I thought..." Janey pauses, but the next words are already in her throat. "I said I thought it was better like that...if she needed the money...to keep it in the family and all..."

"In the family?" His voice is soft, whether in fury or defeat she can't tell. Little patches of pink mottle his face and neck. "In the family...that's what you said?" She sits very still. Something will shatter or tear if she moves. The blood will burst forth from his skin; the very air will come apart. She waits, almost not breathing, for what will come next.

But what comes is...nothing. Nothing at all. He doesn't speak, and she doesn't, and after a while she finds herself thinking of what she will feed them for supper and of how, first, she might walk down to the milk store. (They have a pay phone there, behind the ice machine.) Inside her, emptiness reigns and with it, a touch of something else, rather like relief. Surely, the worst that can happen has happened. Nothing so terrible will need to be said again...

Ahead of them the steel girders of the Jacques Cartier Bridge arch into the ashy sky. The highway has become crowded with cars, and Karl negotiates the lanes with fierce concentration. He hasn't spoken since they left the old road and crossed the Richelieu River. The children have finished slurping up their juice. The rattle of the heater is the only noise inside the car. This is the moment to reach over and lay her hand on his arm. It's what usually happens. She rails at him in one way or another, and then eventually a worn but familiar spirit of reconciliation takes over, and in spite of everything, she reaches out to him. This is that moment. She could touch him like that now, admit that it isn't altogether true about the house, that selling it to the cousin is just a possibility her mother mentioned...

"I'm hungry." Peter's voice is a bleat. "I want a hot dog."

"You can't be hungry, darling." Janey speaks automatically. "We'll be home soon. See the big bridge?" Her hands have not moved. She looks down at them—they huddle motionless in her lap—and knows that the impulse for mercy is not in her any more.

She is still staring at her hands when the sound of snuffling reaches into her consciousness. She turns her head to glance at Peter, but he is gazing out the window with peevish sang-froid. It is Sally Jane's face that has crumpled. Tears are sliding down her beautiful cushiony cheeks.

"Why, darling, what is it?" says Janey. She unfastens her seat belt and twists around to reach into the back seat. Surely the child cannot have understood the import of what has taken place. "Don't cry. Tell Mummy."

"I cou'nent see the rabbits," whispers Sally Jane.

"What rabbits?"

And then Janey realizes. Her stomach curls sickeningly around the knowledge. As she stretches out her hand to stroke Sally Jane's tear-wet face, she looks back over her shoulder at Karl. Is that comprehension gleaming in his pale eyes?

Does he see, then, what she sees? For in her mind has sprung the vision, as clear as the bridge ahead, of rabbits. Grey rabbits and white ones. A whole colony of bunnies hopping about just beneath the icy surface of the water. She can see their ears and their quivering noses, their alert foolish tails. She can feel how it must be under the water, there in their magic summer world. The wash of sunlight on summer grass and the warmth of the fluff that lines their nests, the unearthly softness of their fur...

She stares at Karl for another instant—but who knows what he sees or doesn't see—then turns back to her child. What she wants, more than anything at this moment, is to take the little girl into her arms. She wants to hug away the image that is so compelling and can never be. She wants not to say what she now must say.

KARL'S STORY

He's been driving down this road forever. He's almost sure of this...even though the steering wheel still feels cold in his hand. Another blast of wind shakes the little Chevy, and his eyes flick to the rear-view mirror. Neither child appears in his line of sight. Probably they're already slumped against the windows, bored into semi-sleep.

If he could, he himself would be at home stretched out on the living room couch, which is more comfortable these days since the springs have begun to sag. There's a game on, but it's the warmth he craves and the careless, timeless, cushioning arms of the sofa where he would prop his head on the pillows and ask himself for the fiftieth time whether it is possible for him to go to a party and not grab at everything in sight...the cognac, the pot, his boss's arm, the hungry eyes of the black-haired girl from his office. Francine...he thinks again of dancing face to face with her, of how his body felt warm inside the rhythm of whatever noisy tape Jacques produced to fuel the party.

Beside him Janey has been rubbing her forehead. "All that cognac," she says now. Her voice sounds as though it's being dragged from her throat. "...And Jacques making those geriatric runs at the girls from your office."

"It was a party," he tells her. Ahead of them, a portion of the highway has been repaved. He can see the new crisp white lines, the abrupt transformation to blackness. The car won't rattle so insistently after they reach it...

"My head hurts," Janey says. "Right where cognac always gets me." Again, he hears that roughness to her voice. His own head feels clear, if oddly empty. "...I told Eleanor we had a lot in common, she and I, I mean."

"Jesus," he says warily, "That needling bitch?"

"I think I meant that you and Jacques were a lot alike."

Karl glances at her. Jacques is his boss, an amusing enough guy...but his reputation as a womanizer has reached comic levels. "That's another charming idea," he says. Her long, acorn-coloured hair has caught in the collar of her coat. The corners of her mouth are white and pinched, as though the wind lashing at the car has somehow sucked the heat from her face.

Past her, on either side of the road in fact, fields stretch in barren displeasure to a horizon of scrub trees. Farmland...though it's hard to imagine anyone making a living out of such faded earth.

Karl grew up in a farming community, east of Montreal in one of the so-called Eastern Townships. His grandfather was the minister for several small, rural Presbyterian Churches...they're United Churches now...and Karl remembers the farmers, their faces furrowed with passive anger. These are the kind of fields they worked, sand-coloured, and dry, giving back little for the labour they absorbed. Now, in November, they're unplowed, most of them, and ragged with last summer's cornstalks.

Maybe the riverside will offer more appeal...at least, for the children. Peter is always game for an expedition, and this morning even Sally Jane seemed keen on seeing the rapids. Probably she thinks they're some sort of gigantic waterfall.

"Were you smoking stuff too?" Janey's voice startles him.

The repaved section of the road has already ended; the car has begun to rattle again.

"I saw that dealer friend of theirs over in the corner," she adds.

He nods. "I feel like I've been driving down this road forever." Thinking of the way the road goes on and on, grainy and grey and slightly humped near its centre line, he almost misses her next shot.

"...that black-haired girl? She was smoking too. The one who hung around you all night and did that dance with the lamp?"

His skin prickles. Did she overhear him kidding Francine? Since Nicole, he's careful around Janey. But of course last night's gathering was largely an office party, and everyone in the office knows about Francine and Jacques. "She's one of Jacques' new assistants," he says carefully. What the office doesn't know is that Karl once went to bed with Francine...somewhat before Jacques, as it turned out, and probably a number of other men in the office, if the rumours are true.

"Well," says Janey, "she certainly was having a good time with you."

"Come on," he says in what he hopes is a forbidding voice. "Lay off, will you?"

He remembers Francine undressing to the music of the Stones, her big conical breasts, rigid with silicone as he was soon to find out, the matted fur of the rug she insisted they lie down on. Eventually (he doesn't remember how) he got his own clothes off. He was so drunk he couldn't feel much of anything, and he was never exactly sure how things went after that or even how long he stayed, except that he does recall trying to knot his tie in the elevator mirror and noticing a livid streak of what must have been her makeup smeared like a bruise across his chin and cheek.

"She's like that," he tells Janey now. He can still see Francine's energetic black hair spread, vivid as a crow's wing, against the whiteness of the fur rug. "A party," he adds, "is just a party."

He met Janey at a party. Back when he'd just moved into Montreal from Scotstown. He remembers spotting her in the crowd, her round-cheeked face, the fall of her brown hair, and thinking that seated over there on the sofa she resembled nothing quite so much as a nesting bird. He spent some time with her that night, but it wasn't then that anything particular got started, as he remembers. It was the weekend a month of so later, when she invited him up to her parents' country place.

The first evening she took him out for a walk. They circled the ice-rimmed lake and then, as the sun was setting, clambered together up a steep ridge that rose out of the forest behind the house. Earlier, from the woods and the road, only sections of the house had been visible, glimpses of half-timbered walls, tall windows, high sloping roofs. Nowhere had there been a clear look at the whole.

But, from up on the ridge, he had the view he'd been seeking. Standing there in the glittering, unstable light, he dusted the dirt and bits of granite from his hands and thought that the house beneath them resembled a benign old giant presiding over trees and water. A rather worn and bedraggled giant too. He could see how the stone chimneys canted and how the lines of the roof sagged. The years had done damage. No question. But what a house. His throat constricted as he gazed down on it.

"It's a great place." He slid a hand under Janey's sweater and drew her to him. Against his fingertips, her skin was warm and slightly moist. "I'd love a place like this...land...a real mansion. You must love coming back here." He remembers her face aflame in the sunlight as she turned and gazed up at him for a moment, then slowly nodded.

The next afternoon, she drove them from village to village, skimming along back roads past lakes, through woods. At the time he had been once in his life to Toronto and the Niagara Peninsula, once to Vermont, and though he hadn't yet admitted it to her, the Laurentians seemed to him both wild and exotic. The hills of granite marched northward in rocky profusion, strung with tangled woods and gouged with lakes. And these rough waterholes, still encircled with necklaces of ice, bore the names of French saints...as did many of the villages nestled by their shores and on the slopes of the hills. On the streets and in the shops where they stopped to pick up bread and milk for her mother, he heard French more often than English.

During the ride, she undertook to explain about her relatives. That morning a half-dozen individuals, uncles and aunts as far as he could figure, all of them grey-haired, all wearing shapeless khaki pants and huge sheep-coloured sweaters, had converged on the house. Affable enough over pots of tea, they had nonetheless talked from start to finish about nothing and no one he knew.

"They just assume everyone knows everything about them and about the lake..." Janey said in a tone that might or might not express regret. The car was proceeding...much too fast, he felt...along a narrow, tree-darkened road. Only loaf-shaped mail boxes standing at intervals along the way betrayed the presence of houses deep within the thicket, though occasionally he glimpsed a pale sliver of lake through the web of leafless branches.

"People don't bother me," he told her.

She negotiated a gravel-spitting turn, then took one hand off the wheel to push back the wing of hair that was obscuring her cheek. "They're really sweet. It's just they're a bit feckless...except for my father, of course."

He stared at her. Her parents were ridiculous people. How could she not know this? Feckless was the exact word. Her father especially. Stalking around the room like an actor, while the fire smoked and sank.

Yelling his way through the evening news. The man was nothing but an old blusterer...though it was clear he frightened Janey.

Later in the afternoon they stopped for a beer. He still remembers sitting opposite her in the wooden booth. Her straight shiny hair slid forward across her cheeks, and from time to time she shook it back, smoothing the long locks with the tips of her fingers as if she liked the feel of her own hair. He had the sense he'd had at the party, that she might at any moment take to the air and in a whir of wings be gone.

They were sharing a plate of poutine, a dish consisting, as far as he could tell, of French fries and cheese curds awash in gravy, and with it drinking pints of whatever was on draft at the bar, and she was telling him once again about her family, most of whom seemed to be retired from, or entirely without, occupation. "They've all got places around the lake. Four aunts...and uncles of course...and my cousins too, some of them. I was the only only-child." He drank his beer in slow cool swallows and listened. It seemed important that he should know this history. The aunts were her father's sisters. There were stories, of trains missed and recipes gone wildly awry, of guests arriving on wrong nights and strangers taken in as old friends. In the flow of her voice, calm began to permeate him. He told her a little of his own story, the weekly gestation of his grandfather's sermon, conceived in melancholy silence, readied for delivery amid spasms of rage (neither he nor his grandmother spoke above a murmur that last day; the worst beatings had always taken place then too, though of course these Karl didn't mention). He talked about his grandmother's kitchen, the stove he'd kept stoked for her, the big enamel-covered table where he'd studied, the pots of porridge and coffee and the thick winter soups, potatoes and carrots and legumes, that his grandmother had kept at a slow steam on the back of the stove. He described his own habit of befriending small wild animals; pets had been forbidden him thoughout his childhood. And as he talked and she talked and the afternoon went on and on like another road opening out before them, he began to imagine that she was falling in love with him...the way she listened with brooding intensity, the way her eyes followed him when he got up to get them another beer, as if he gave her leave to breathe.

That night in his room, he spent several minutes standing at the open window. A misty crescent of moon dusted the sky with a faint light, and the uppermost branches of trees were jagged rents in the luminous charcoal of the sky. The air smelled of ice and old leaves.

When finally he turned back to his room, it seemed for a second that the moon had entered the room. He blinked. The flutter of white dissolved, became an angel standing in the doorway. The angel, of course, was Janey, afloat in a long white nightgown, her curved hand shielding her flashlight as though it were a lit candle. For a second they held like that, suspended, he would have said, between the window and the door, until she moved toward him, and he gathered her in, pressing his lips quickly against her mouth, partly to keep the silence (he could not bear to lose the moment), partly because he did not think that he himself could speak at all. He could feel the warmth of her even before his arms folded around her.

Only he could take care of her. He decided this while he was still making love to her. Only he...and he was almost sure of this...only he had the will to rescue this house and this family, preserve these sloping roofs and cavernous halls, these bannisters and beams and ill-lit rooms, crammed most of them with objects inherited...of however little value, it didn't matter. It didn't matter either how much her father yelled or her mother snivelled. Adept for many years at shutting out voices, he hardly heard them.

Beneath him now she whimpered, a soft eerie sound that might have come from somewhere outside, and for a second their walk earlier that evening came back to him. Tired of her father's ranting...by then her mother was weeping as well...he'd pulled Janey out of the living room, then out-of-doors entirely, and together they'd made their way, hand in hand, skidding and sliding, down the slippery path to the lake. Almost in front of their feet, a rabbit had skimmed across the wet leaves, and even as she'd squeezed his hand he'd found himself wondering what animals might live in these woods. Besides the usual racoons and foxes, deer maybe, and even bear. The thought had seemed oddly possessive, as though these new woods were his to know, and now, as he buried his face in the wealth of her hair, the knowledge flashed into his mind, quick and sure as the rabbit darting into view, that he meant to marry her.

"I talked to that man Rowan for a while," Janey is saying. "Sort of pompous..."

"Oh, he's okay...just the kind of guy who goes after things," he says. Isn't it Rowan she got stuck with that time at the agency dinner...back when Karl himself had just been transferred into communications and Rowan was the hotshot up in retail and fast foods? The guy talked her head off.

"We should have a party," she says. "We've been to Eleanor and Jacques' a million times."

"Sure. Why not?" Up there...is that the entrance to the park? Probably. A pair of denuded trees marks a stone gateway. Quite often out driving he's not too sure how far he's come, even on routes he travels often.

"I want a hot dog." The high, querulous voice is Peter's.

Janey shifts in her seat to look back over her shoulder. "We'll have a snack after we see the rapids," she says.

"See rabids," comes Sally Jane's murmuring voice, and Karl feels his heart lurch. Sally Jane has strings around his heart like no one else does. When he talks about her, his voice goes husky, and sometimes, looking down at her as she hauls that giant stuffed bunny around the apartment, he can't believe how much he feels. Only three years she's been in his life, and yet he can't imagine being alive without her.

For Peter his love turns more on the question of responsibility. He plays with the boy nearly every evening, catch and throw and street hockey mostly. But these games have the flavour of training and preparation, of combat even. He feels the need to fortify his son, to ready him for the battles ahead. He wants, he would say, to make a man of him.

"Rapids, love," says Janey. "We'll be there soon." Karl can feel her glance swing back to himself. "A party with some of your office people, some of the ones I've met at Eleanor and Jacques'. The black-haired girl, for instance..."

He stops breathing for a second, then says in a neutral voice, "Francine? Sure, she's good fun."

"And Rowan maybe...?"

Relief flows through him. "Why not?" He glances at Janey for an instant. She's very thin these days, and older-looking, despite her regrown long hair. Now, he thinks suddenly, her features have changed. A new glint marks off the planes of her face; new shadows have enlarged her eyes. She's gotten better-looking somehow...he would tell her that if she asked...it's just that she no longer looks like a girl.

His affair, by which he doesn't mean rolling around on the fur rug with Francine...his real affair happened at a time when he'd just been made an account executive. It was a job he'd aimed at since the beginning, one he already knew he would do well. He could see the parameters of the entire agency by then...and nowhere to go beyond them. Montreal was not big enough, the major government accounts too deeply planted in the francophone side of the business. He could see just how far their own, mostly anglophone agency would get, just how far he himself would get. Unless he wanted to move, and he didn't, the future was all known, all attainable...and then Nicole walked into his office.

Rangy and tall, she was then nearly forty. Her husband, much older than she, had been a scion of one of Montreal's first families, and she'd inherited a portion of his family companies, one of which had just been assigned to Karl. Nicole spoke languages, Spanish and Italian, as well as French and English. For a hobby she bought antique furniture and china, and she wore clothes like no clothes Karl had ever seen. White and beige and pale gold, colours that were hardly colours. Even draped over motel furniture, her silk shirts and cashmere dresses, the slippery bits of underwear she'd tossed off like bons mots, seemed as rare and finely wrought as the objects she treasured.

Naked, her body was that of a long-limbed animal...taut and sinewy, stained with old tans and scarred as if from old battles across abdomen and diaphragm. In bed she was languid as a cat in the sun and, so far as he could discover, without inhibition. "Why not?" she would say in the same husky, light-hearted voice she might use to greet the offer of another glass of wine. He was, she told him, the best-looking man she'd ever slept with, and the fact seemed to please her greatly, as if she'd found him, undervalued, in one of the Sherbrooke or Crescent Street shops she frequented. By himself, he stared into the mirror but saw nothing except the skin he shaved each morning, the mark on his chin where a stray dog had bitten him years ago, a pair of ice-coloured eyes that stared back at him, as they always did, without a hint of recognition.

The first glimpse of Nicole striding through the dim reaches of some bar or restaurant always startled and then excited him...as if he'd found himself suddenly in a new and more remarkable world. The shine of her clothes and her white-toothed smile, her leisurely voice as she greeted him, seemed to clothe him in superior raiment. He could feel all around himself the stir of interest, and in the afterglow of her arrival, he sometimes imagined an alternative history for himself... private schools and travel, noble or at least notable relatives, an ancestral manor house of improbably beautiful proportions.

He began, that year, to feel he was two people. He had only to walk through the apartment door, and any recent hour spent in bar or bed with Nicole disappeared from his mind. Loosening his tie, dropping his briefcase onto the kitchen table, he paused to watch Peter zoom his little metal cars across the floor. With equanimity he met Janey's dark-eyed stare as, baby straddled on one hip, she glanced up from sink or stove.

"You look too good," she said once, when he'd just come in from a rendezvous, and he experienced a shock like an electrical charge up the back of his neck, as though she'd reminded him of some fearful danger he'd forgotten.

She herself looked exhausted. Shadows had pooled under her eyes during those first months after Sally Jane was born. She still fell asleep sometimes in front of the television, and a few weeks ago he'd come home to find her slumped at the kitchen table, eyes shut, head resting on a section of the newspaper while Peter played at her feet.

"Whatever that means," he replied, making his voice casual. He took the baby from her arms. The smell of pork chops filled the kitchen; even the baby's shirt reeked of pork and garlic. "Let's eat soon," he told her. "I'm hungry."

"Twenty minutes..." She'd recently had her hair cropped, and her freed hand stroked the back of her head, as if it was searching for the missing hair. "By the way, that guy never came to fix the radiator. Do you think you can fix it, bleed it, or something?"

The smells of home, the concerns of home...this was his life. So how could there be a Nicole in it? At the office, he recalled the burnished look of her hair and clothes, he imagined the sounds of the languages she spoke. But even then she was like a woman he'd read about or seen photographed in a magazine, someone glamourous and removed, about whom he'd thought from time to time, with fleeting greed, as any man might, what would that one be like to fuck?

"It had nothing to do with you." When he said this to Janey, he meant it. He expects, sooner or later, to erase the fascination he sometimes still feels. (Nicole is living in Rome now; he can picture her in silk the colour of champagne, seated in some piazza among the ancient, beautiful buildings whose photographs he has studied.) The affair after all was so happenstance. If, for example, he hadn't taken that afternoon to go with Nicole to Quebec City, perhaps he wouldn't have gone to bed with her at all. Or, if the cleaners had not meticulously returned the objects left in his pocket, perhaps Janey would never have known. He thinks now, however, that her finding out rescued him. The choice was so clear...and so easy for him to make. He felt then, and still feels, as if he emerged, not exactly unscathed, but more firmly and precisely himself. If anyone has changed in the aftermath, it is Janey. He can't pinpoint the difference, but it's there, and sometimes, observing her, he is afraid.

"That's fine then," was what she replied. "That makes me feel just fine." He remembers the ragged edge to her voice and how, behind her, he could see the green-striped curtains she'd made to match their bedspread and, through the window, the brick wall of the apartment building across the lane. The words of apology, of love, caught in his throat, and for a minute he thought he would choke. Only after Peter came wandering into the bedroom and he'd picked him up and held him to his chest, did he manage to speak. "I'm sorry," was what he said then. He remembers clutching the wiry narrow body of his son and staring, through the wisps of hair they could never brush down, at Janey...her face looked blurred as though it was wrapped in a fine mesh...and he knows that at that moment he was afraid he was going to cry.

Here at the river's edge, the wind comes straight off the water. Like invisible knives, it harrows the brown grass, slashes at the trees and the bushes. "Bloody freezing," says Karl, thinking again of the couch, of coffee and the mindless bombast of the football game. Sally Jane clings to his jacket as he sets her down.

Janey nods. "It's too late in the year." Bending her head against the wind, she takes Peter's hand, and together they head toward the water.

Karl gets Sally Jane set on her feet. She takes a step forward, then staggers slightly. Maybe he should carry her; the ground looks uneven all the way to the river. He bends to pick her up, and at that instant she takes off. His shout leaps after her into the wind.

For a three year old, she is unbelievably fast off the mark. More than once Karl has wondered if she would make a good sprinter, even imagined himself travelling to track meets, dispensing priceless fatherly advice...these thoughts crash through his mind as he races after her...that icy water...

The capture is swift, almost as swift as Sally Jane's feet, which do not slacken their pace even as she nears the water's edge. As his hand closes on her shoulder, he can see the plunging water, the silver-edged rivulets snaking between the rocks.

"Sally Jane! Honey...!" Another two steps... "Don't do things like that..." Bending to speak directly into her ear, he hears his heart thumping inside his chest. "Never again honey. You hear me?"

He can feel her oblivion. He can feel too her unyielding desire. Deaf to his words, she strains against his hand. If she could, she would leap from his grasp into the water itself.

Still gripping her arm, he stands up and stares for a second into Janey's shocked eyes. "Christ," he says. "What's got into her?" He glances out at the river. In that frigid, fast-running water, he might not have had the strength, might not have had the endurance...he shrugs away the unbearable thought.

"Is this the park?" Peter is tugging on Janey's hand.

"Yes," she tells him. "Yes, it is the park. But it's colder than we thought, isn't it?"

He nods solemnly, and together the four of them move to the river edge. Still in Karl's grip, Sally Jane leans out over the water. On her other side Janey squats down and slides an arm around the little body. She whispers something, then with her free hand points toward the rapids and speaks again. Her voice, which he can barely hear, has the tolerant, coaxing tone of a teacher, and he suddenly sees her as she must have been, sitting at her desk, facing a bunch of kids, her cheeks flushed, her eyes bright with concern. It is the first time he has pictured her at work. "...The rapids come from stones that are just underneath the water," she is saying. "You can tell where they are by the little white waves. See the little white waves?"

Sally Jane nods. Then she twists around and glances up at Karl. "Daddy?" she says. "Daddy get 'em?"

Bending over her round, hopeful face...her cheeks and her nose are pink from the cold...he hates the need to shake his head. "Daddy can't get them. The rapids aren't something you can have. They stay in the water." For a second he fears she will cry, but she merely turns back to the water, as though she can't bear to keep her eyes off it. He straightens up then and glances at Janey. "You've got her?" She nods, and he lets go Sally Jane's hand.

Long ago in Scotstown, if he cried, especially if he came home crying, his grandfather caned him and then made him go out and stand in the old garage at the back of the manse property. Men, even small ones, didn't cry. Though the pain has disappeared...he can't remember a single blow...his grandfather's face, eyelids compressed, lips flared with contempt, hangs over him still. The beatings were swift, the banishments life-long, it seemed. Now, as he stares down at the intent figure of his daughter, the dank cement smell of the garage fills his nostrils.

They had no car. His grandfather borrowed the doctor's stationwagon to haul groceries and to call on sick parishioners; his grandmother didn't drive. The garage housed various implements, most of them mended, as well as the winter's wood supply, and Karl endured his confinements sitting on the chopping block (he was supposed to stand, but he could hear the groan of the garage door in time to be found standing rigidly at attention).

In those hours of chill and darkness, he thought about how it would feel to hold a small animal in his lap. Kittens, from time to time, ran half-wild in the field behind the garage. It was easy to imagine gathering in one or even two of the little striped creatures. He would wait until the right week and then wean them from their mother, tame them with food stolen from his grandmother's pantry, keep a box of sand and a bed for them hidden in his closet.

A dog took over his imagining at another stage. The doctor's spaniel bitch had recently whelped. There were five liver and white puppies in the litter; one had crawled all over him when he went to visit, licking the palm of his hand and chewing on his fingers. This round and wriggly little character could, he was sure, live secretly in his room.

Other times in the garage, Karl tried to imagine his father returning to claim him. But what kind of father? A man in a car? A tall man? A man with a mustache? His father had never, Karl now knows, been married to his mother. Earlier than Karl can remember she moved to the city to work; twice or three times a year she reappeared at the farm. All through his childhood, she did this. He has a photograph of the two of them standing in the field behind the house...a small child with dark hair and eyebrows and a diffident, possibly rather pretty girl, frowning at the camera. She looks more like an older sister than a mother. Within a day or two she was always gone, usually after a screaming battle with his grandfather. Karl's father was later killed in an accident...or so Karl was told. He has never exactly believed this, but the older he's grown, the less inclination he's had to check.

The year before he graduated from high school, his mother married a filling station owner from Alberta. This man had two grown daughters of his own. He was, and is, as far as Karl knows, a nice enough individual. Karl and his mother exchange letters twice a year, and she sends the children each a Christmas present as well, usually something too small. Janey's teary, doting mother has been their only grandmother.

On the way home Janey gets out cookies and cans of juice for the children. "For Christ's sake," Karl says as she's popping the can tops, thinking of the spilled juice, the crumbs wedged into the cracked vinyl. "We'll be home in half an hour."

Ahead of them a row of river houses has swung into view, and he studies them now, one after the other. Flanked by evergreens and manicured hedges, the houses stand at the foot of sweeping driveways. They are so large and elaborate, each of them, so serenely old-fashioned, he can imagine them in the summers of long ago. The lawns would have been dotted with white-painted, wooden furniture, the kind that wedges itself into the turf. There would have been children and dogs romping down the grassy slopes, and out on the river, stately old ChrisCraft launches coursing up and down the waterway, their brightwork gleaming, their captains hailing one another...

He takes a deep breath. "If I get that wholesale marketing account," he says, "and you go back to teaching next year, we could think about buying an old house." He glances at Janey, then back toward the river. The house up ahead is a Tudor affair, stuccoed and half-timbered. From this distance it resembles Janey's parents' place. "Ask your mother, and your father, what they think."

"They're going to sell the house." Her voice slashes across the space between them. "They're selling it to my cousin...the one who lives in Europe. He wants a place to come to in the summers. My mother wants to keep it in the family..."

He feels a surge of pain so great that for a second he can't draw breath. It's as though she's knifed him. "She could have told us..." he manages.

"She did..." Again that voice, "I mean, she told me, last weekend. She asked me what I thought. I said I thought it was better like that...if she needed the money...to keep it in the family..."

The hum in his ears alarms him. He visited Niagara Falls once...his whole high school class...they travelled all night in a bus...and what he remembers most of all, even more than the river and the wall of crashing water, is the noise. A doomful roar that engulfed them as they stumbled out of the bus more than half a mile away...long before they could see the cataclysm itself or even knew in exactly what direction it lay.

"In the family? That's what you said?" Beside him Janey doesn't move. Her face, with its new pallor, looks frozen.

The bridge looms now, its steel girders arching into the paler steel of the sky. Since they left the river road, he's been doing battle with the traffic, eyeing the other drivers like enemies, gunning the car from lane to lane.

"I'm hungry..." The voice is Peter's. "I want a hot dog."

"You can't be hungry, darling." Janey's voice bears no resemblance to the rapier that issued from her mouth a moment ago. "We'll be home soon. See the big bridge...?"

She's the children's mother after all. Nothing can change that; nothing can change the fact that they are, the four of them, a unit... A sniffling sound comes from the backseat. Sally Jane. He knows her voice even when it's no more than a whimper cast adrift in the middle of sleep.

Beside him Janey unfastens her seat belt. "Why darling, what is it?" She twists around to reach into the back seat. "Don't cry. Tell Mummy."

"I cou'nent see the rabbits."

The whisper enters his consciousness and hovers there. What can she mean? But already he knows. Rabbits in the river. Not the lean skittish creatures he used to spy on in the fields behind the manse, but rabbits as she would see them. Fluffy, lettuce-eating...an underwater kingdom of bunnies waiting for Sally Jane to come and kneel among them and stroke their fur with her baby hands.

"What rabbits?" says Janey. She pushes the hair off her forehead and extends her arm into the back seat. Then her eyes swivel to lock briefly with his. Surely, he thinks staring at her, they can still do something. There's a pet shop near his bus stop...he can build a rabbit hutch; he's got the tools...

The car shudders, and he tightens his hold on the wheel. A fierce cross wind is sweeping the bridge span. At the same time he hears Janey clear her throat, and, as he learned to do long ago, he closes his ears. Against the trill of voices, he thinks of the rabbit's fast-beating heart, of how it will pump against his chest as he stands in the apartment doorway holding the little creature in his arms. He can see the joy springing in Sally Jane's face, the flash of her legs and her wild feet as she leaps toward him. Yes, a pet rabbit will fix things.

Ahead, a series of exit signs swings into view. Their own will be one of the first, just after the foot of the bridge. Casting a fast look behind him...Janey is blotting Sally Jane's cheeks with a kleenex...he edges the car into the far right lane, then glances at his watch. Maybe, if he's lucky, there'll be just time to catch the last quarter of the game.

If only the delusion hadn't gone on so long...that's the pity of it, he thinks now, that's the waste... if only they had understood sooner.

TESSA

Tessa paused in the doorway to her bedroom. Clothes lay everywhere. Her clothes. Unhemmed some of them or with seams pulled apart. There were magazines too, scattered across the quilt, and plates and glasses, and shoes and hangers, but no scissors. She stood fingering her bangs. How was she to cut her hair? Get rid of those horrid wisps of white she had just spied in the bathroom mirror?

At her feet a pile of dresses suddenly moved. "Robert?" In the silence of the house, her voice was startling. The pile mounded nearly to her knee and then sank.

She knelt and reached beneath the dresses. A paw, soft as a flower, batted her hand, then subsided as her fingers located the hard little skull. The warmth of the furry body passed into her hand.

"Silly Robert," she told the dresses. "Silly, silly Robert."

She spent another moment manipulating the blanket of skin over his shoulders, then stood up. Now, if she could just think where she had put the scissors. Brushing the hair from her eyes, she reached for the glass of sherry that stood on the dresser. Answers...answers.

("Somebody might as well tell little Tessa the answer." That was what her daddy used to say, and to this very day she could feel the weight of his hand on her head, hear the boom of his heavy laugh. He was so thumpy loud, her daddy. So big and daddy powerful. But he wasn't here now to tell her the answer. There had been that terrible day and then no Daddy at all...and no Mummy either, of course.)

An answer came to her not ten minutes later, just as she was tying her new red scarf, an answer not about the scissors but about her biggest problem. And it seemed so right, this answer, she wondered she hadn't thought of it sooner. She would kill Robert. Not, of course, Robert the cat. But Robert her husband.

It was the perfect answer. And the perfect day for it too. Robert's body wouldn't be discovered until after the weekend. It would lie rotting in his apartment...yellow with some virulent poison or crimson with blood... She took a large swallow of sherry.

Robert, her husband, had left on one of those warm, dark September evenings past the equinox...a darkness made of velvet, thick enough to muffle the sound of his car pulling away from the house.

It was the detergent bottle filled with sherry that had set him to packing. He'd discovered it while he was looking for the stain remover; the bottle had sloshed too vigorously for detergent. The last straw, he'd called it. After all he'd done, and not done. The drugs and the doctors. Keeping her at home when they'd wanted to send her to that hospital again. He'd pointed all this out. And now he couldn't take anymore. He'd told her that too. Not caring... But here she shook her head. Of course, he cared. He was a man of deep sympathy. People confided in him, unhappy people, women especially. He liked to help them. So, when he saw how she felt, realized her despair, of course he would change his mind. He would come back. He would come back or else...her hands gave the ends of the scarf a sharp tug...or else she would free herself of him, and soon too. She would finish dressing. She would look in on her sleeping daughter; like any teen-ager Sandra loved to sleep away Saturday morning. Then she would feed Robert and be off.

Sandra's door swung wide with a gentle creak. Early morning light gleamed off polished floorboards, bare as always of rug or litter. It touched with silver fingers the uncluttered surfaces of desk, bureau, chair, and lingered like a benediction over the sleeping figure on the bed.

The figure stirred, then sighed and sank again into stillness. Tessa held her breath, recalling with sudden thirst, the small, trustful Sandra who'd held onto her mother's hand, who'd loved the games and the puppet shows and the gay little songs. They'd been like two little girls cavorting beneath the benevolent gaze of Robert, Robert smoking his cigarette, occasionally from his considerable height offering them his guardian's smile.

But the Sandra of today was a big girl. Across the room her inert body lay, broad and solid, in the centre of the bed. A body unquestionably the product of Robert's genes. For Robert had not only withdrawn himself, he had taken the child too, infiltrating her body from the inside out...so that she had grown up calm and strong and a little clumsy, fond of injured animals and needful neighbourhood children, a rescuer and a caretaker. Her room was like a clinic or a temple. Carefully, for who could step across such a threshold, Tessa shut the door.

On the way down the stairs, Robert zoomed past her ankles. He detoured through the living room, then caught up with her at the doorway to the kitchen. This room, he implied pushing past her again, was his territory. "Feed me," he mewed, flowing around and through her legs, nearly tripping her. "Feed me. Never has a cat suffered so much."

"You're such a pig," she told him as she poured a measure of the dry catfood into his bowl. "Such a bloody pig." But Robert was not listening. Already he had buried his greedy young cat's face in the bowl and was nosing through the food. The crunch of catfood was the only sound in the room.

While he ate, she poured herself a glass of sherry from the apple juice bottle and drank it down, measuring the spread of heat in her stomach. Only an inch or so of the beautiful golden liquid remained in the bottle...

Not enough! She blinked away the flash of panic. There was the bottle in the laundry room and the one in her bedroom and two in the storage closet...or had she drunk one of those? Another in the shoe box. There was enough. Robert, grandly pouring out the contents of the detergent bottle, had not guessed at the magnitude of her supply.

In the St-Henri quarter of the city, the wind seemed stronger. It lept at Tessa as she emerged from the car. The trees in the square across from Robert's place bent swishing and complaining. Leaves, some of them brilliant shades of red and yellow, rushed over the grass, and while she stood in the street collecting the folds of her coat, dark clouds tumbled over the sun. In the sudden shadow, she shivered. Robert would not consent to be killed, after all. Might he not do something to her, hurt her? (Her daddy had hurt her mummy, though her mummy had not of course been so little and dear as Tessa.) But it didn't do to think of that. Bending her head against the wind, Tessa hurried across the street.

Robert's apartment was on the top floor of an old house. The construction was very fine. He had explained this apologetically, as though otherwise he might not have left home. He was fond of structure. Balance was another thing he craved. And peace and quiet, of course...

The door of his apartment opened as she reached his landing. Strains of a Mozart concerto drifted down the hall, and Robert's large head peered around the door frame. She took him in at a glance. Her Robert. His broad nose and thick hair, half grey, half brown. The old cords he was wearing. And the shetland sweater, one she had given him years ago. A rumpled man, indistinct somehow, even faded. Worn-out in fact. Why, he needs me, she thought. He must.

Robert, however, did not sound as if he needed her. "What is it?" he was asking in the careful tone he used when he recognized that she had been drinking.

"Let me in." She was still panting slightly. He made no move to release the door. "Let me!" He looked at her for another second...her willingness to make a scene always alarmed him...and then wordlessly backed away. She darted inside.

As he shut the door, she bounded across his entry hall and into his living room. He took a startled step after her, but she had stopped already and was staring around the room. Whatever had she come for? There was no one in here, not even one tiny girlfriend. Oh, yes...but she should have brought the scissors. Or a knife. She should have brought a knife.

"There's no one here for you to scream at." He had come into the room behind her. Now, as she glanced round, his hand moved to his shirt pocket and produced a flattened pack of cigarettes. He looked so discouraged that she turned away.

There across the room, like an old friend waiting, sat the sofa from their basement...and in the corner, the ragged armchair that had been little Sandra's favourite place to play house. The rug, however, was new. Tessa studied it. An oriental in muted colours, the kind of colours Robert would pick. Or maybe his newly acquired girlfriend, the lady accountant whose husband had treated her badly, maybe she had picked them. Beige and blue and a pale sand shade. Yes, accountant colours. In the center of the rug sat a glass coffee table which was unfamiliar too, and on this stood a small framed photograph of the three of them, Sandra, Tessa, and Robert, all staring straight at the camera. It was the one he had decided to take away with him the night he moved out. He had wrapped it in a pair of socks. "Happier times," was what he'd said by way of explanation, as if his leaving her was some sad but necessary decision. She should have killed him right then.

"I'm taking that home," she announced. He had just managed to light the deformed cigarette he had extracted from his pack, and now, instead of speaking, he exhaled a stream of smoke. She glared at him.

"What is the point of this?" he said finally. The cigarette rested on the centre of his lower lip, in a sort of hollow. Smoke floated up the middle of his face.

"It's my picture. I want my picture..." She heard her voice rise toward a scream. His features tightened. For a second he looked as though she had hit him...but just for a second...and then he got hold of himself. She watched him produce his smile (without losing the cigarette), his guardian's smile.

Deep in her chest, the desire to kill him grew stronger. Dead, he could be scraped off her. The endless cloying support offered without love, the mess of his broken promise. For what was the failure to love her, her of all people, what was it but a broken promise? He had loved her. Of that she was sure. He had been enchanted by the darling girl whom everybody had loved. And then...and then it had collapsed. She never could tell how. Her little needs, her little woes, her little problem with the sherry. And the problem grew bigger after that. How could she stop herself while the love...because, of course, he had loved her...the love had been tumbling down around her in shreds? And here she was now, trapped in a great pile of ruined love. No wonder she needed him dead.

In the meantime he remained standing before her, smiling, saying nothing.

"I want it back." She would need a gun.

His hands came slowly out of his pockets. He took a drag from the cigarette. With his other hand he pushed back his ragged hair. "I'd like to keep it," he said, "To remind me of better..."

"Don't say that," she cried.

"What am I supposed to say?" he asked.

She could feel him, holding her off, yet hanging on at the same time. He withheld himself. He withheld everything, but he wouldn't let go. She pointed at the photograph. "The camera can steal your soul. I read that somewhere. And that's what you did, isn't it, Robert?"

"Look," he said, "We'll go back to Doctor Edelmann. I'll take you back to him. He'll help you."

"Didn't you, Robert?"

"It wasn't even my camera," he told her and blew out another stream of smoke. "I didn't even take the picture. Remember, I'm in it too." He gave a little snorting laugh and then smiled at her, willing her to share the joke. "Somebody else stole your soul. Old Freddy or whoever took the picture. Or you lost it yourself."

She bent and picked up the photograph from the coffee table. Such a little face. The childish bangs, the dark hopeful eyes. Standing between the two big people, her husband and her daughter, how small and almost negligible little Tessa looked. The stone of her engagement ring ground easily into the glass. The sound was a thin scream. The smile flew off Robert's face. His features jerked as if she were scratching him. Twice she drew the back of her hand across her own face leaving an X etched into the glass.

"For Christ's sake, Tessa!" he shouted as she flung the photograph onto the sofa.

"There," she said. "That's what you want, isn't it, Robert? Then you can say you don't know how it happened but little Tessa just got crossed out..."

A length of ash fell off the end of his cigarette onto the new rug. He stared mournfully down at it. "Look," he said, not lifting his head. "Just look a minute. This isn't getting us anywhere." He bent to collect the fallen ash. "We'll go out...have a cup of coffee. We can discuss this," he added standing up again, the ash cupped like a communion wafer in his hand.

He was desperate to get her out. She gazed at him a moment. She could throw something (there was an ashtray on the coffee table), make a really big scene. On the other hand, to go out with him... "Giorgio's?" she bargained. It had been their favourite neighbourhood place.

"Giorgio's," he said instantly. "Giorgio's it is. We'll each take our own cars." The relief on his face was obvious, but still...she would be sitting across a table from him. They would be a couple. Things would feel better. Maybe he would buy her a drink.

He bought her a coffee; she decided to be pleased, to imagine he was coming back to her. And indeed, mightn't he? Mightn't he see?

"Such a cheerful place," she remarked, and to prove how charmed she was, what a delightful companion she could be, she glanced gaily around at the wooden tables and panelled walls. Plants hung in the window frames. Along the glass counter top stood rows of big jars, full of dried fruit and coffee beans from Africa and South America and teas from China and India and Ceylon (though there was no Ceylon anymore, was there?). Giorgio was phasing out the dried fruit, introducing home-made pasta. He explained this as he led them to a table.

He brought them mugs of dark, steaming coffee, then spoons and little paper cups of cream and a bowl filled with envelopes of sugar, and finally, as if it were a further and delicious tidbit, the bill, which he laid gently beside Robert's mug.

Robert dug two envelopes of sugar out of the bowl. "Look," he said when Giorgio had left them. "Look, it's not that I don't want to see you. You know I'm concerned. I want to help. But these surprise visits, wrecking things..." His thick fingers tore through the envelopes. Sugar sprayed around his mug. He shook his head.

"What you need to do," he said dumping the remaining contents of the envelopes into his coffee. "You need to rebuild your life. You need to quit drinking. And you need to go back to Dr. Edelmann. I'll take you back." With his napkin he dusted the sprayed sugar into a careful pile and swept it into an ashtray. His face had taken on an expression of benevolence. Didn't he always look like this when he was fixing something? In another minute he would give her one of his smiles again. "This summer I'm lecturing for a week at the Institute. In London. You remember?" He smiled. "You can take your holidays then. You and Sandra can come over and stay with the Arthurs in Warwickshire. I'll come up for a weekend. You'll get a good rest. You'll..."

She stopped hearing. His mouth continued to form words. You see, she said, speaking in her mind to an invisible listening god, you see how it is? He'll never stay, and he'll never go. I ought to have done it. "I was going to kill you," she said thoughtfully.

His eyes jumped away as though she had shot flame at them. "Now see here..."

"I thought of it this morning," she explained. "I want to be happy."

He nodded. He understood. "Of course you want to be happy." His hands, as he placed them on the table, were shaking. "We all want to be happy, but..."

At that moment she suddenly put her hand on his. She didn't mean to. He was so unkind to her. She didn't mean to touch him at all. But it happened. Her hand crept over the back of his. Oh, it made her want to cry. That timid little sandcrab of a hand. "But we were happy," she assured him, pressing the pads of her fingers against his skin. "We really were. I know we were." He looked at her, his mouth still open to speak, and started to nod. Then his mouth shut. His eyes slid away from her gaze. Slowly he shook his head. The thatch of his tweed-coloured hair quivered.

"No," she cried. "No, don't shake your head! We were happy! Remember?" He was peeling her hand off his. "Don't do that!" she cried in a panic.

He glanced around, but no one seemed to be noticing them. "The truth is I thought I was the fix-it man. Dr. Edelmann made me see..."

"Stop it," she begged. "Please stop it."

"But I was wrong. I couldn't..."

"No, no, don't say these things."

He shook his head, vigorously this time, as though he were shaking her off. "The truth is I should never have married you."

"No!" she cried. "No. We were happy. We could be happy."

"You aren't listening," he said. "You never do."

"We were happy. Don't you remember? We must have been." Why, that very morning, when she'd looked in on the sleeping Sandra, the division between the happy past and today had been so marked. As sharp and differentiated as the passage from hallway to bedroom. She'd been able to see, in the light that hovered over her sleeping daughter's body, just how things had been.

Across the table his big face blinked slowly into focus. "You mustn't say things like that," she told the face. "You mustn't. Why, you've taken up years and years of my life."

"It was my life too," he said.

After a minute he lit a cigarette. For just a second, he looked like a person in pain; then smoke poured from his mouth and nostrils blurring his features.

Around them in the room, a bustle had arisen. People had been drifting in from the shops along the street, demanding sandwiches and slices of quiche to take out. Some had seated themselves, like Tessa and Robert, at the wooden tables.

"I was such a lovely girl," Tessa said now, more or less to herself. She pressed her fingers to her forehead. Her head hurt, her chest too. "Someone should have loved me," she said.

Robert's face came toward her through the cloud of smoke. "Now, I don't want you to think that you can't depend on me..."

She stood up. "Giorgio!" Her voice, high and girlish, pierced the chatter. Lunch customers lifted their faces. Forks were suspended, coffee mugs lowered. "Giorgio, please...bring me a glass of sherry!" She glanced around at her audience, overtly acknowledging their interest. Like children called to attention, they gazed up at her.

"My husband has just told me that he should never have married me," she told the enthralled faces. "It's all been awful for him. From the very beginning. And it's all over...although, of course, it never was...and I must rebuild my life." Fingering her scarf, she nodded graciously at them. "Actually I'm not alone." Her voice came out clear and almost conversational. "I have a daughter. And I have a cat. I named the cat after Robert actually...so there would still be someone named Robert in the house. I...." She stopped because Robert had now risen to his feet as well. Not looking at her, he stubbed out his cigarette.

The five dollar bill he dropped floated down and landed on the bowl of sugar envelopes. Then he was past her, stuffing his wallet into his pocket, grabbing his jacket from the coat rack. All the eyes that had been on her now swung dutifully after him. He bumped a table. He kicked into a chair. His jacket sleeve upended a glass. Finally he reached the door and wrenched it open...the rush of wind hit them all...and then he was gone.

In the silence that followed, Tessa's audience suddenly discovered a collective embarrassment. Quickly the faces turned back to each other. Even before she had dropped down onto her chair, she could hear little desultory remarks bounce back and forth at the tables. Everyone in fact seemed to be talking at once. Only Giorgio appeared unruffled. He brought her a glass of sherry and another bill, bowing as he backed away from her.

It wasn't until several minutes later, as she was sipping her sherry and trying to think what to do next, that she noticed Robert's cigarettes and car keys. Huddled beside his mug under the shelter of the first bill, they seemed at that moment like orphans, pets or children, that he had left behind.

Outside, car keys in hand, she peered up and down the sidewalk. Her throat burned from drinking the rest of her sherry all at once, but the pain inside her chest had eased.

It had rained evidently. The pavement was wet. Leaves stuck in untidy patches to the sidewalk. Robert was nowhere in sight. His empty car, another of his orphans, sat parked across the street directly in front of her own. Probably he had gone for a walk. He often did when she had upset him.

The car, his car, took her carefully over one of the big bridges out of the city. Once she stopped to buy gas, and a little while later, feeling her own emptiness, she pulled into a shopping centre. A deli with a big red cash register sold her a sandwich. They sold coffee too, in styrofoam cups, but she decided against more coffee. And then, when she came out of the deli, there, just as if it were meant, right next door, was a nice new liquor commission fronted with the familiar purple and white sign.

After that, whenever the traffic was light...that is, when no cars were near enough to see into hers...she took a quick gulp from the new bottle. The rest of the time it sat like a friend along for the ride, conveniently propped up against her purse, on the passenger seat. Clouds slid across the sky. The occasional gust of wind shook the car. The pavement dried up, and smears of pale blue appeared in the sky. Late in the afternoon she became aware that the car had doubled back and was heading for a bridge into the city.

"No, no, not yet," she admonished it. "But soon."

No doubt it was missing Robert. Poor Robert, wandering along a sidewalk somewhere, looking this way and that, his head wreathed in smoke, attaching objects and people to himself, then casting them off again, unsure of what he wanted and where he was going. Near the bridge she suddenly wrenched the car off the highway and onto a tree-lined side street. Should she crash the car or merely abandon it here in this unfamiliar suburb? She decided on the latter course. A crash might hurt someone else, a passerby, or a tree. The car itself might be hurt. "Only the guilty should suffer," she said aloud. The words buzzed like flies around her ear; she had to open the window to get them out of the car.

In the end she left Robert's car in the parking lot of a school. She decided against leaving the keys in it. Someone might be tempted to steal it, and there would be another crime. Leaving the new sherry bottle, nearly empty now, in the car, she set out to walk to the bridge.

By the time she reached the river, the sun had slid low in the sky, and she was shivering. Soon, very soon, it would be evening. In the cold air she already could imagine how it would be in the coming darkness, how the lights of the cars would slash through her. They whooshed by now. Lanes and lanes of cars; the sidewalk seemed barely wide enough to walk on.

Part way across the first section of the river, she stopped and leaned on the railing. Long rays of sun lay along the surface of the water, the light changing imperceptibly from gold to bronze and then almost to red while she watched and watched. Gazing down at that light, she hardly felt cold. For a long time she dangled Robert's keys from the iron post. When finally she flicked them off, they dropped without a whisper to the great cement pilings below. Almost immediately after that, as if in natural sequence, she was able to flag down a taxi.

Minutes later, as they swept across the long bridge...she could never have walked the whole of it, she realized...a ruby glow rose from the river and filled the air and the sky above the bridge. She could feel this light like a faint wind, as though it were blowing up from the surface of the river.

"My how beautiful." She sighed and leaned back slowly. The driver glanced in the rear view mirror at her but decided evidently to say nothing. She could see down river now, all the way to the next bridge. A river of red glass. I could stop the taxi, she thought, I could get out and jump, and the river would shatter when I hit it. But she made no move. Indeed, with her back pressed into the car seat, she felt now that she might never move again.

She was asleep when the driver's voice roused her. "How far up the block, missus?"

She sat up and peered out the window. "The next stop sign," she told him. Her mouth was dry as cloth. "Just beyond the stone wall..."

Her house pulled up and stopped beside them. Leaves brushed over her feet as she got out of the car. More leaves swirled up the side of the house. They'd had the bricks pointed last year, the shutters repaired and painted (although in the dimness she could barely see these improvements), and it was Robert who had bought the antique brass knocker. All this before he'd decided...whatever it was he'd decided...that he would move on and improve or repair something and somebody else. Leaning back into the cab to pay the driver, she felt tremendously tired. Her little hands could hardly pull the wallet from her purse.

As she came into the house, Robert the cat rose from the hall chair. He stretched up in a curve that resembled a question mark and came forward to greet her as she hauled off her coat. His languid steps meant that he had been fed recently but would nonetheless be willing to down another serving. When Tessa didn't respond to this offer, he took his usual executive decision and followed her to the kitchen anyway.

The note was propped up in the agreed-upon place, a corner of the kitchen table. "I've gone to Rosemary's for the night," it read. "Homework all done except for math. Daddy came and borrowed your extra car keys. Love, Sandra—P.S. I'll do the math tomorrow at Rosemary's."

Just when the idea of killing Robert turned back on itself, Tessa wasn't sure. Perhaps it had been the river, but she didn't think so. More likely the note, supported there between the salt and pepper shakers. Or the silence of the house. All dusty and thick, like old curtains over her face...a silence so heavy she couldn't hope to push it back now.

She drank off the last inch of sherry, then refilled the decanter from a bottle in the storage closet. She knew what to do. But first she would cut her hair, get rid, yes finally rid, of those cruel white hairs.

Closing her eyes, she pictured a falling leaf—its lacy spine and delicate, desiccated skin curling ever so slightly inward at the edges—but this leaf didn't slide to earth defeated. Oh, no. This leaf flitted here and there, and then, on a final thrust of the wind, it simply rose and sailed away.

And wasn't that just how she felt now...a wisp of nothing...as if her daddy had come and picked her up and whirled her in the air? (The same as he had done to her mummy, whirled her in the air until her head hung that funny sideways way.) Now she could feel herself float up and up on her daddy's powerful laugh. Still with her eyes shut, she tried raising her own arms. Yes, with the littlest push from her feet, she had certainly floated there for a second. The fur gliding past her ankles was the only reminder that she still remained near the ground.

"Oh, Robert," she said aloud, opening her eyes and glancing down at the cat as he oozed over her feet. "Do you know he took my dear little car...that too?" As she spoke, her knees buckled and her elbows and forearms smacked down onto the counter. The blow brought tears to her eyes. And struggling upright, she felt, as she had in the morning, that she had better hurry.

Upstairs in the darkened hall, she fumbled through the various objects crammed into the linen closet. Her fingers located the scissors finally by the expedient of pricking her finger on the points. But it was Robert, insinuating himself through her ankles, who caused the fatal accident. They had started back down the hall together, with Tessa carrying the scissors, points downward in the approved way like the good little girl she had been, when he stepped between her feet.

Somewhere in the background, she heard his furious yelps, and then she was falling. Pain stabbed through her hand and her chest, and outside the moan coming from her own throat, she heard, or thought she heard, a gristly, tearing sound. No further yelps pierced the darkness of the upstairs hall.

(Yes, upstairs was where her daddy had gone, up, up the stairs, carrying her mummy, all dangly over his shoulder. The little Tessa, sitting cross-legged on the living room floor with her paper doll and all those fidgety paper doll clothes, had heard their door shut, crunch, and a few moments later, the noisy, hurtful bang. And the little Tessa had torn up those paper doll clothes...ripping and ripping them until they weren't clothes at all. That's what the little Tessa had done.)

Beneath her breast now, the wet mound wriggled slightly. Like a fur baby, she thought. Warm liquid slid cozily between her trapped fingers, dry tufts of carpet pressed against her lips and cheek. Robert, poor Robert, she wanted to say, poor Tessa, poor Robert...but no voice, no sound at all came to lift the silence that crowded the hall. And then, just as the mound beneath her stopped its wriggling, she had the happiest thought. Perhaps if she took a pill or two, got into bed...Robert would come. He would find her there sweetly sleeping, and then he would see how dear and needful she was. He would come back and take care of his little Tessa.

Sandra, returning shortly after nine that night to fetch her forgotten math book, discovered her mother reclining on the unmade bed. Tessa lay gracefully arranged among her unravelled garments, one hand flung back behind her head, the other trailing off the edge of the bed. She was dressed, and a red scarf peeked jauntily forth at her throat. Her blouse, from collar to waist, was dark with blood.

Sandra did not run or scream or do any of the things a teenage girl might be expected to do, having come upon such a scene. Her voice, informing her father over the telephone that her mother had been murdered, sounded calm.

Robert, arriving simultaneously with the police car, found his daughter seated on the window sill in her mother's bedroom. While the police were bringing in their equipment, he suddenly offered her a cigarette. He had lifted his hand as if to smooth her hair, which had no need of such attention, and instead had pulled the pack from his pocket. She rose to accept his offering, then held it to his match with a hand as steady as his own. They remained like this at the far end of Tessa's cluttered room, heads mutely bowed together like a pair of refugees.

The police, had they chanced to glance up from their labours, might have recognized the expression on the faces of father and daughter as one of shared exhaustion. The police, however, had other things to do. It had taken them only a moment to establish that Tessa was not dead. Neither had she been stabbed or shot, as they'd all assumed. With the ambulance on the way...they could hear the rising howl of the siren...a brief search of the bedroom turned up an empty decanter and an equally empty box of valium lying companionably side by side under one of Tessa's dismembered dresses. She had left no note.

The body of Robert, stretched along the side of the unlit portion of the hall, its blood caked into the dark carpeting, was not discovered, as Tessa had predicted, until after the weekend.

AFTERNOON AT THE BELLERIVE

The Baronesa de Montenegro pauses at each apartment door. The light from the chandeliers is so faint she can barely make out the numbers. Still, she is not displeased. That antique brass cage of an elevator. This hushed and spacious corridor. Even the dimness seems a proper reticence. She peers at a number. Ah, yes, this is the one. She raises her hand and knocks.

A moment or more of silence...the Baronesa does not knock again...then the rasp of a bolt, and the door opens to reveal the meagre figure of Nanny. Behind her, another, smaller figure is moving about among the furniture. The room itself is awash in light from a pair of tall windows. In the glare the Baronesa recognizes the predatory curve of her aunt's back (the women in the family are prone to dowager's hump) even as the figure pivots on its walking stick. Aunt Luisa. The last of that generation.

"Nanny!" The old voice, at least, is strong. "Do stand aside! My dear Isabel, how splendid..." The walking stick thumps the rug.

"Yes, yes...do come in, dear child...my lady, I mean." Nanny's voice too, unchanged. (Their father always swore the bleat of Nanny's London voice gave him a headache.) "I didn't recognize you there for just that minute..." Speaking, she has let go the door and now backs abruptly into the room, and into Aunt Luisa.

"Donkey!" cries Aunt Luisa jerking back and attempting to rap Nanny's ankles with her stick.

"Here now," says the Baronesa in a voice she would use on her grandchildren.

The stick misses its mark. Nanny staggers and recovers. Her hands clasp together in front of her chest. "Well, excuse me, I'm sure. I'm sure I meant to bump you like that."

"Donkey," says Aunt Luisa again, but with resignation. Her free hand brushes the seams of her dress in slow disdain, as though Nanny's touch has left some residue. The Baronesa steps into the room and closes the door behind herself.

Bending, a moment later, to kiss each papery cheek, she inhales the familiar smells...mint and mouthwash from Nanny, lily of the valley from Aunt Luisa (that old, luxurious scent from Patou)...and without warning the aunt's dressing table sweeps into her mind. As if they are before her, she sees the objects scattered over its mirrored surface...crystal powder box poised on silver legs, perfume bottles like miniature decanters, brown-stained around their stoppers, exuding the aroma of lilies.

Yes, that was how it happened...she can remember herself, the uncertain young woman who sat at the dressing table while Aunt Luisa stood behind her wielding the big silver hairbrush, grooming her protegée for the meeting with the eligible Montenegro. Even now, she can almost feel the sweeping brush strokes, can almost hear the resonant voice, seducing her young self into confidence.

"...Over there, my dear." The same voice is speaking now. "On the sofa. You will have a splendid view if this tiresome fog will lift.... Nanny, do be of some use. She does not wish to hold her coat all afternoon."

The voice then... "Who has allowed you to butcher your hair in this manner? Nanny have you been at it with your shears?" And then, as now, the bleat of protest cut short. "No matter. We will do what we can...so, with this barrette." The sensation of hands lifting her hair from her neck, the unfamiliar weight of it piled high on her head. "There, do you see? Hair, my dear Isabel, is an aphrodisiac. And perfume...it is important to understand...perfume is not a crime. Nor is mascara. With a nose of such character, one needs eyes... Nanny, bring my cosmetics case, the white one, from my dressing room. And my jewel box...those poor naked lobes!"

That advice opened the door to her whole future. The Baronesa has always believed this. Without her Aunt Luisa's counsel, without the loan of those seductive accessories and the allure they implied, the Barón would never have been persuaded. Bribed or otherwise induced by her father to come calling, how would he have believed, gazing at a girl so plain, whatever it was that he needed to believe in order to choose her? That she was a girl not only well-born, but confident in the offering of herself. A girl serene in her naiveté, ideal for a man of thirty (himself even more well-born).

The Baronesa gazes tenderly at Aunt Luisa. They say she is no longer reliable in day-to-day matters. Not actually senile, but she confuses the generations. Though just now, it must be said, she looks not the least bit confused. She has been settling herself in the opposite corner of the sofa, patting down a sleeve, plucking at a ruffle. Her smile, as she gazes back at her niece, is perfectly alert. "On a fine day, my dear, you would be looking straight across the lake to Evian. A pretty view...though the town is become a dull spot these days; they have closed the casino, you know...." She waves a dismissive hand in the direction of the window. "A pity there are only the mountains."

The Baronesa nods. Above the layers of mist piled in the hollow of the lake rises a range of Alps. From this angle she can see several snowy peaks. Magnificent, despite the mist. She would certainly say so if asked. Yet...

"Aunt Luisa?" Her voice sounds sharp to her own ears. "The curtains, Aunt. The glare, do you not think? It is quite impossible to see within the room as it is." She waits out the slow rotation of the old head.

"The curtains?" says Aunt Luisa and then begins to nod as she gets the point. "Yes, yes, of course. You are not accustomed to the light. Nanny! Will you draw the curtains, then?" Nanny hangs her head for a second, then veers toward the window.

In the pause which follows, the Baronesa holds her eyes resolutely away from the view. He will not leave her. She knows that. And yet... She fingers the gold buttons on her suit jacket, glances down at her skirt. Such foolish thoughts chase through her head...how the folds seem almost to have arranged themselves...how this surely is the value of a superior house, a true maison de couture...how perhaps the girl will die...

Aunt Luisa's voice summons her back. "Well, my dear, it is good of you to find the time to visit me. I know you and the Barón..."

"Us," says Nanny from the window. "Visit us." She releases the inner set of curtains and then the outer. The heavy layers of satin and velvet fall together, banishing the glare. All three women blink and glance around as if awakened from a spell. The interior of the room has leapt into view. And what an interior. Since the Baronesa's last visit, an explosion of objects has taken place. There are now six of the ornate old

Louis XV armchairs, each choked with plump little cushions, and over by the wall yet another sofa of the Empire style, covered in an opulent purple and gold striped brocade. There are ormulu encrusted commodes and bureaux plats, two étagères crammed with collections of Sèvres plates and bowls and another full of silver snuff boxes and those tiny Meissen porcelains, pug dogs and musical monkeys.

"That will certainly do, Nanny," says Aunt Luisa. "Now do settle yourself." She inclines her head toward a wing-backed chair. Nanny, after one rebellious glance which the aunt appears not to notice, tacks around several laden tables and makes for the chair.

The conversation must, of course, continue to be held in English...for the sake of Nanny. The British do not speak other languages. Moreover, both aunt and niece have spoken English from their respective nursery days...other languages being as much *sine qua non* as good manners and couturier clothes. By languages, of course, one meant the tongues of western Europe, though in the recent generation the Baronesa has noted a flurry of interest in modern Greek on account of the young Queen and her brother. But in the old days, the mastering of French and Italian came first, then German and English. The Baronesa, indeed, learned her first English from Nanny. Much later (by then their accents had been corrected), she and the other children were made to read widely in English...poetry and even novels. At one time, Hemingway was said to be a friend of her father's, although the Baronesa doesn't remember him ever coming to their house...so perhaps the famous American writer was merely an acquaintance. Such stories from the past are often, she knows, distorted.

"Would you like your tea, my lady?" Nanny is lowering herself into her chair as she speaks.

"Of course she wouldn't," says Aunt Luisa. "She has barely arrived. She hasn't..."

"I asked," retorts Nanny. "No more than simply asked. Some people..."

"But tell me," interrupts the Baronesa. "Tell me news from the family. I am a terrible correspondent myself. Even my children complain."

Both old women pull themselves erect. "Let me think," says Aunt Luisa.

"There was that letter from Concha," offers Nanny. Her gaunt face emerges from the shadow of the chair's wings.

"Yes, yes, the dear child's daughter is marrying the grandson of Bienvenida. That is quite right."

"A good family," says Nanny judiciously. "Though not a patch on ours, my lady." She beams at the Baronesa.

"The English uncle?" Aunt Luisa says now as though they have been speaking of him all along. "What was his name...oh, yes, Broadfoot. He has died of a heart attack...some months ago, I believe."

"That was two years ago," says Nanny.

"And the youngest Cáceres had a frightful car crash," continues Aunt Luisa. "Now what was his name? Alphonso? Antonio?" She adjusts the scarf at her throat. "He recovered, I believe, or...no, that was the other one." She nods to herself.

The Baronesa, who knows neither the Broadfoot nor the Cáceres in question and does not particularly wish enlightenment, merely nods and waits.

"She doesn't know them!" Nanny pounces. "That's not her side."

"Nonsense," replies Aunt Luisa. "They sent me more of the furniture and silver from that estate. I can't use it, of course. And lace. I have never worn lace. But she was a good child." She tips her head in the direction of her niece. "You knew Rosa. You spent summers with her children more than once."

The Baronesa smiles. "Yes, of course. Rosa. Certainly."

"Your father always liked to have the extra children. He said it made your mother happy," Aunt Luisa tells her now.

"Did he?" says the Baronesa amiably.

"Kept her busy," says Nanny. "That's what he was after."

Aunt Luisa turns on her. "You!" she says. "You knew nothing, remember; your business was with the children."

"I knew a lot," sniffs Nanny. The Baronesa stares from one to the other. Both old faces gleam with malice.

Strange. When the family pensionned off Nanny and sent her to Lausanne as companion to the old aunt, the solution seemed ideal. After all Nanny had been devotion itself back all those years ago when Aunt Luisa came to live with them. The Baronesa remembers the tragedy that brought her. Uncle Santi, killed while racing his Bughatti on the Haute Corniche. Aunt Luisa, swathed in black veils, arriving with her trunks and trunks of clothes. Nanny, though ostensibly still in charge of the younger children, had spent half her days rushing about on errands for the elegant young widow, paying emergency visits to the chemist, the perfumery, the glove-maker, delivering notes and invitations. Whatever has happened to all that eager servitude?

"You knew nothing," Aunt Luisa is saying. "I assure you. Nothing at all."

The Baronesa draws a deep breath. "Tell me, Aunt, do you find the climate here suits you?"

Aunt Luisa, with obvious reluctance, turns her gaze back to her niece. "The climate?" she repeats. "Ah, yes. It does suit. Always fresh, really quite agreeable…"

"Too damp," says Nanny and begins to rub her wrists.

Aunt Luisa's head snaps back. "Why do you not return to England then? No doubt the perpetual fog would suit you."

Nanny's head withdraws turtle-like into the shadow. Her voice darts out from the depths of her chair. "And who would run about for you and do your messages? Those chocolates you like so much. And what about Pedrito? Who would take him out then, I'd like to know?"

"Pedrito?" asks the Baronesa. Surely they haven't got a child here? She glances around the room.

Aunt Luisa raises her hands and claps them several times. "Ven, Pedrito!" she cries in her rich voice. "Ven a Mamita."

There is a scratching at one of the side doors and then a single high-pitched bark. Nanny gets up and clumps across the room. "Useless creature," she says angrily. When she opens the door, a black poodle of the toy variety dances into the room.

"Aquí!" cries Aunt Luisa, and the dog quick-steps across the room and springs sharply into her lap. His curly head settles into the folds of her stomach. His pom-pom tail beats wildly.

"Mi pequeño," says Aunt Luisa fondling his ears. "Mi pequeño niñito."

Nanny shuts the door so hard the Sèvres plates rattle in their stands. She sniffs in the direction of the dog and then glances meaningfully at the Baronesa. "Gets worse every year," she says. "Your father…now he would never have allowed a mangy little creature like that into the house. Never. A fine hunting dog, those big German ones, that was the kind of animal *he* liked."

"Qué bonito," croons Aunt Luisa. Her parchment features have taken on an expression which is nearly coquettish. Her crooked hands travel from the dog's head down his neck. Hungrily, she strokes his back and shoulders.

"Your father," says Nanny turning ostentatiously toward the Baronesa. "Now he was a gentleman...the old school." Her smile reveals ragged brown teeth. "And you begin to look like him, my dear lady. The nose and the same black hair, I do believe."

The Baronesa, whose hair colour has long been the responsibility of her hairdresser and whose nose is large and aquiline, is not amused.

"Yes, indeed," says Nanny agreeing with herself.

It was a joke back then...Nanny always gazing after Father, quoting him, sighing as he strode away after a visit to the children's quarters. The Baronesa closes her eyes momentarily. She can see Father now, not the features of his face, but the shape of him standing in the street while men loaded the trunks into the first taxi. A man stiffly tall, with a cigarette in a holder, the smoke rising around his face. And beside him Mother in a pale travelling suit, a soft hat shadowing her eyes. At the last moment, while the driver of the second taxi stood holding the door, her mother turned and came back up the steps to kiss each of them goodbye. The Baronesa can feel again the fuzzy hat brim brushing her cheek, can almost recollect the smell of Mother's hair as she whispered her goodbye, the inevitable admonition to be good. But all the while, over Mother's shoulder, she was watching Father, master of everything and everyone.

Never would he have conducted himself as her husband has lately done, never have placed their mother in such a position. "Do you remember the time they went to America?" she asks her aunt suddenly. "The year before I married, the year they took the train? My mother had never seen that country. He described to all of us where they would go. You remember?"

"Yes," says Aunt Luisa. "Yes. The breadth of that continent. It was a long trip for those days...the trunks of clothes, weeks and weeks of..."

"*I* went with him," interrupts Nanny. Her avid old face emerges from the chair. "I caught the next train and met him in Paris. We took the ship from Cherbourg."

"My father?" asks the Baronesa, her voice rising on a note of disbelief. Has Nanny gone mad?

Aunt Luisa makes an exasperated face. "Pay no attention," she tells her niece and then begins to laugh. Her face cracks into the thousand broken lines of a puzzle.

"You didn't know!" crows Nanny. Her long cheeks quiver. "No one did. I said I had to visit my family in London. He was mad about me."

"It was nineteen hundred forty-eight," says Aunt Luisa. "The Americans were holding their presidential election..."

"Six days to New York," says Nanny. "I had a new coat..."

"A Mr. Truman," continues Aunt Luisa in the tone of one conducting an eminently reasonable conversation. "He was a haberdasher, I believe, quite unsuitable...and a Mr. Dewey..."

"He bought it for *me*...a beautiful new coat, big as a cape..."

"You must stop this," orders the Baronesa. "I will not have my father spoken of in this manner."

The aunt glances at her niece in surprise. Then, after a few seconds, she begins to nod. "Yes," she says. "Do go ring for tea, Nanny. You are being tiresome."

The Baronesa uncrosses and then recrosses her legs, in the process turning exclusively toward her aunt. Nanny gets up and goes muttering to the telephone.

"She cannot help herself, my dear Isabel," says Aunt Luisa. She smiles and strokes the sleeves of her dress. "But my, I do remember those days so well. Your father was a great traveller. What they called an adventurer..."

"Tea," insists Nanny into the telephone. "Apartment three-one-seven."

"He always needed to know more..."

"No scones?" complains Nanny. "We always have scones..."

"He wanted more." Aunt Luisa's hand stroking her own sleeve has grown limp, her expression thoughtful.

When the tea has been consumed, Aunt Luisa instructs Nanny to reopen the curtains. As in the opening moment of a play, the parting of the heavy folds of drapery catches each of them. A blade of light slices open the room. They hold their breath as the gash widens, and in an instant, reality has transferred itself to the outside. The Baronesa rises to her feet. She too must get outside.

As if by the same compulsion, Aunt Luisa is struggling to her feet as well, and together, while Nanny goes to fetch coats and leash, they stand, aunt and niece, staring out the window. The mist that earlier hovered at the very windows of the hotel has retreated to the centre of the lake. Directly below them, the garden beckons. Shadows extend from the stunted trees and underline clumps of bushes. Flowers tinted with new light glimmer along the base of the garden wall. The sun has very nearly broken through.

"Oh, do look at the swan!" says Nanny.

The three women have occupied a bench near the low stone wall that marks the shoreline. With the dog lashed to one of the slats of the bench, they sit in a compact row facing the lake. Flaps of Nanny's tweed coat and Aunt Luisa's loden cape reach like restraining hands across the Baronesa's lap. Trapped, a little girl between her nanny and her aunt, she sits very still, staring straight out at the lake. Speckled with birds, it undulates gently before her.

"Yes, indeed," says Nanny, "Just look at him. Swans are the finest bird..."

"A snake in feathers," says Aunt Luisa.

Directly opposite them a few feet out from shore, a particularly large swan has cleared an area of water. The other birds...ducks of many varieties, a number of smaller white birds, and gulls as well...have moved off to less disputed territory and are swimming about and occasionally diving alongside the stone jetties. The swan paddles in circles before his audience. Alternately he picks at feathers on the back of his neck and plunges his head into the water. Once in a while he glances toward the three shore-bound women as though he knows he has entranced them.

"And the Barón, my lady?" Nanny's voice, like one of the gulls, swoops out over the water. "Did he come with you to Lausanne?"

"He is at this moment giving a speech, I believe...at his conference," replies the Baronesa still gazing outward. "I came to Lausanne with him because I wished to see you both." She utters this partial untruth calmly. She has already used it on her husband.

In fact, although she is glad to see Aunt Luisa, and Nanny too, she has come along primarily to prevent the Barón from bringing with him his current mistress, a young woman of uncertain and, therefore, undoubtedly déclassé background. Informants have not been lacking. He has taken up dancing and nightclubs again. He refers to the girl, when travelling with her, as his nurse.

The Baronesa has never until now doubted the true substance of her life. As a husband, the Barón has been willful but seldom unkind. Where she has been inclined to gravity, he has been light-hearted, sometimes shockingly cynical, yet always indulgent of her concerns. He has chosen, with taste and decision and occasionally with surprising perspicacity, schools and companions and even spouses for the children, clothes for himself and for her, the furnishings and paintings for each of their dwellings, not to mention the dwellings themselves. Though he has conducted other affairs of the flesh, still as the Barón's consort, as the mother of his children, she has felt herself secure through all her adult life, in a position of honour...like her mother before her.

But not like her mother now. Not like her after all. For the Barón has done what her father never did. He has been crude and obvious, and people know. This is the horror of it. They know, and they are all talking. A nurse indeed! And travelling with him openly!

A shameful wish rises like nausea in the Baronesa's throat as she gazes out at the swan. Let the girl drown. Or better. Let *him* suffer. There would be justice. Let him sustain a crippling blow, a stroke or a heart attack. Let him have a real nurse.

"Ah, the young Barón," says Aunt Luisa warmly. The Baronesa, stares at the aunt. The "young Barón" is in his seventieth year.

"Not so handsome a man as your father, of course..." Aunt Luisa is adding. "Still...the same sort of man. Appealing to women. A man like that can hardly help himself." She pushes out her lips and gives her niece a look which is both shrewd and sympathetic. "Your mother, fortunately, understood him well."

"She never knew about me though," says Nanny, leaning across the Baronesa's lap toward Aunt Luisa. The dog, disturbed by her motion, shifts position.

"Donkey," snaps Aunt Luisa. "There was nothing to know." The Baronesa stares straight ahead.

Out on the lake, a light wind flickers over the water. Streaks of black and blue and grey mottle the swaying surface. The swan thrusts his head into the swell. Aunt Luisa gathers the green cape about her shoulders. Stiffly she shifts her weight and straightens her back. The bench quivers with her exertions; the walking stick slides to the pavement. It has already done so twice before, and automatically the Baronesa bends to retrieve it.

"I am quite chilled," says Aunt Luisa, taking back the proffered stick. "Thank you, my dear."

"Thin blood," says Nanny, whose own nose has turned rosy above her tweed collar.

At this point, just as Aunt Luisa has drawn breath to reply, three little girls rush shrieking past their bench. Aunt Luisa transfers her attention to the flying trio. "So young," she remarks, staring after them. Her tone is not one of envy.

"We should go back now." The Baronesa punctuates this statement by rising. "There is a reception at the conference...for wives as well. I do not wish to keep my husband waiting, naturally."

"Why ever not?" says Aunt Luisa. "You are too humble altogether. Especially for one of your station." She leans forward and, smiling up at her niece, plants her stick firmly between her feet. "Your hand, my dear. The chill has stiffened my knees."

When they return to the apartment, a waiter is clearing away the tea things, gathering scattered napkins and cups, dusting crumbs from the table tops. Pedrito issues a series of sharp barks and rushes at his ankles.

"Stupid!" cries Aunt Luisa turning on Nanny. "You have let go his leash. You know he cannot bear finding a man in these rooms..."

"Filthy beast," says Nanny trying to step on the trailing leash. The hotel servant shakes his foot at Pedrito, who backs up shrilling his disapproval.

"Shut him in that bedroom!" orders Aunt Luisa.

Nanny stoops and manages then to kneel on the leash. Pedrito interrupts his barking to snap at her outstretched hand. Aunt Luisa looks over at her niece. "He is such a spirited creature," she explains happily.

"But come!" She turns her back completely on Nanny and the furious dog. "As you have said, you must not be late for your husband. Though I cannot imagine why you should believe that. It is far better for the men if they are kept waiting; the tedium refines their appreciation." She smiles, and her parchment skin crinkles. The Baronesa smiles back.

Leaving the two, servant and semi-servant, to deal with the still yapping Pedrito, aunt and niece walk slowly back down the hall.

Wall sconces have been lit along the corridor, and the new,

interlocking circles of light illumine worn patches along the centre of the hall carpet. The Baronesa looks carefully around. The brass of the sconces is stained, the fluting dented. Here and there on the wall, panels of embossed paper have peeled at the edges, revealing strips of plaster. Aunt Luisa, seeming smaller even than before, moves crab-like beside her. Once again the rich, flowery scent of her perfume is in the Baronesa's nostrils. Finally they reach the elevator. A worn patch mars the carpet here too. Beside the elevator door, a red "Occupé" light glares rudely at them.

"It is still properly run, this hotel?" asks the Baronesa. "You are quite comfortable?"

"Yes, yes," says Aunt Luisa frowning distractedly. "You know, my dear Isabel, you were the best of his children. Not an ounce of guile. But you never could laugh." She reaches out and takes the Baronesa's hand. Her touch is dry and cool. "And really, my dear, it is not altogether convenient to live one's life without a dishonest act. The art of dissembling, you know, the occasional well-placed lie..." The crooked old fingers grip harder. "But that is not exactly what I wished to say. At my age, one doesn't know which time is the last, and I wished to..." She pauses once more, works her mouth as if pressing into shape the words she needs, and then speaks again. "The men have always done things in such a way, you know, in our family, among our sort of people... It is not a thing of importance. They have so little to do, most of them. They play out their men's games..."

The Baronesa closes her eyes. Who does not know then?

"One should never suffer by the men, my dear," continues Aunt Luisa. "They cannot help what they are. It is better, if you are so inclined, to play your own game. There is considerable amusement to be had, you know."

The Baronesa feels the heat of tears behind her eyes. "But he..." Her voice sounds to her own ears like a child's. Helpless. "But he is making a spectacle. People know, many people; they feel...sorry for me."

"Oh, well, my dear, but still... Not that sorry. It is not you after all who have played the fool. My own husbands had a number of such amusements. Your father...more amusements...and people knew. They always know." She lets go the Baronesa's suddenly rigid hand and stabs a finger in the direction of the apartment. "Nanny is of no importance, of course. It is merely that her tongue has come loose with old age. She was always a silly woman, even young, and now she is become spiteful..." She stops.

The Baronesa has stepped backward and thrust out her hand. "My mother went on that train trip!" she says. The sensation of imminent tears has disappeared from behind her eyes. "My mother! It was Nanny who stayed home with us children. Naturally. My father would never have done such a thing."

Aunt Luisa peers quizzically at her niece. "Child," she protests, "but of course he would have done such a thing. He did do such things." She smiles to herself. "Although not with poor Nanny. You are quite right about that time." She says this last soothingly, as if being "right about that time" will restore the Baronesa to perfect equanimity. "It *was* your dear mother who went to America. They had a most amusing holiday too...so many tales to tell. He brought back a buckskin jacket. She found jewelry to buy, silver and turquoise and some orange stone..."

"Coral...from the natives," murmurs the Baronesa, speaking through the tumult in her brain. My mother, she says to herself, closing her eyes and calling up the fuzzy hat, the goodbye kiss. But once again it is Father's form she sees. Opening her eyes, she addresses Aunt Luisa. "Everyone knew? That is very hard to believe, what you say."

Aunt Luisa looks taken aback for a second before she shakes her head. "Well, my dear, I suppose one tends not to know one's parents' amusements. But in any case, it simply was not so important a thing." She shakes her head again. "And as for your husband, my dear, you make far too much, really far too much. You will become obsessed...like poor, dreadful Nanny...now there is a case..."

"Whatever *is* the matter with Nanny, then?" asks the Baronesa suddenly. She feels breathless, as though the oxygen has been sucked from the air. Is it possible that her husband's performance can be so easily dismissed, like the behaviour of a naughty boy? "Even if my father...even if Nanny knows things, why must she be vindictive? A fool really...and inventing such a story about Father, pretending?"

Aunt Luisa looks surprised once again and then laughs. "Why, the poor woman was madly in love with your dear father. For years. And now that she is a trifle addled..." Behind her the red "Occupé" light goes out and then flashes on again. "Such an infatuation. Your mother was always amused...poor Nanny. Surely, even you little ones knew?"

The Baronesa nods. "We considered it a great joke. But now that I think of it, she was quite pitiful, really. She must have known well enough then that he had no interest in her?"

"Indeed," says Aunt Luisa. "But, of course, she was young, and she had nothing else in her life. Those English nannies..." She pushes out her lips and frowns, as if over the follies of all who lack her particular wisdom. "They used to come to us in Barcelona, to teach the children English. They never managed to learn decent Spanish, you know. And not one word of Catalán. It was comical...how they prided themselves on their ignorance. As this one does still. There was a community of them, but no men..." Again she points in the direction of the apartment. "I doubt she ever had a man, you know. Nanny was no beauty." She says this complacently.

"No, she was no beauty," the Baronesa hears herself say. Her heart closes hard around the words.

"Still..." muses Aunt Luisa after a pause, and she seems now to be speaking more to herself than to her niece, "Still, she enjoyed my little adventures, you know. The secrets made her feel important, and she was quite useful. Not the treacherous old donkey she is become, braying about the train to Paris. Though it hardly matters now, after all these years. She brought the ticket to me, you know, from him; she was our go-between."

The Baronesa studies the shrivelled face but finds no malice in it. "My mother was the one who went to America," she reminds her aunt gently.

"Of course, my dear, of course. The trip to America...she did go," says Aunt Luisa. "But Paris... In those years Paris was wonderful, the centre of the world. Such a rebirth of spirit after the war, such excitement... The time we managed to meet there he bought me a coat at the house of that new young man, Christian Dior... Poor Nanny must have been jealous. A great voluminous thing it was. The New Look. My..." She sighs, and her short upper lip lifts in a smile that seems, for the moment, utterly unselfconscious and even sensual.

It is a smile the Baronesa has never felt on her own face, yet she recognizes it instantly. It is a smile that tells the delicious and particular joy of being desired. And the light that shines out of the ruined features is the pure, exultant light of youth.

"Did my mother know about you?" she asks her aunt softly.

"Your mother? Oh, perhaps." Aunt Luisa pushes out her lips, thinking this over. "You know, my dear, it was all so lighthearted. I'm sure she didn't brood on such things. She was a graceful woman, your mother, and truly gentle. Even in her death. She died gently. Something broke in her brain and pouf..." Aunt Luisa flutters her crooked fingers to indicate, presumably, the delicacy of this mode of departure. "Really, my dear. The harder fate is to be the one left behind...as I am. And trapped in this dreadful body. I'm sure God is a perfectly dreadful individual..." She leans toward her niece, and her face in the chandelier light takes on a gossipy, confiding expression. "But I will tell you, my dear, though I am still glad to have taken my pleasures where I found them, I did envy your mother. From time to time I truly did...as some may envy you."

"Envy me?"

"I should imagine so, my dear. After all, it is you who truly have him, and you are much the same as you were then. The same lack of artifice, so girlish. It was that which attracted him, you know. Dressed up in borrowed finery...that suit is Chanel, is it not?...you looked so innocent."

Again that sensation of breathlessness. "But it was you who enabled me to...attract him. I have always been grateful. Even now. I could not have..."

"Nonsense, my dear. Of course, you *could* have. You did. He was, as you know, something of a roué when he married you. The most attractive ones often are. And that sort tends to value innocence."

The Baronesa blinks at her aunt. "But he has never...desired me. I am afraid he..." She stops. The words she cannot say fill her throat. I am afraid he will leave me.

But Aunt Luisa is making another of her dismissive gestures. "Even if he had once desired you madly, my dear Isabel...even then, today it would all be ashes." A grimace of amusement drifts across her face. "I can assure you of this, my dear. The memory is pleasing of course, but passion is not a thing which endures. One cannot even keep it alive in oneself. Sooner or later one prefers the children or the dog or those wonderful truffled chocolates..." Her voice slows. "Nanny buys them for me, you know. She has found a splendid little shop...in the avenue du Théâtre..." She pauses...the expression on her face has grown distracted and greedy...and then peers at her niece. "Now where exactly was I?" she says irritably.

The Baronesa draws breath to answer, but already the old face is clearing. "Ah, yes, husbands. Husbands indeed. Yes, I do think, my dear, that you have done an intelligent thing in travelling here with him. Perhaps you are learning." She reaches out suddenly and draws her finger down the Baronesa's cheek. "You do know, of course, that he will not leave you?"

The touch is still dry, but warm now, the pressure fleeting. An angel's hand, thinks the Baronesa...mysterious. "I am afraid that he will," she says. The sensation stays on her cheek.

"Of course he will not!" says Aunt Luisa. "The girl is a mere servant, is she not? Or something of the sort...a nurse? He knows well enough who you are and who he is." She nods and then, in the face of the Baronesa's uncertain silence, shrugs one loden-draped shoulder. As you wish, the shrug implies.

At that second, the little red light beside the elevator flashes off. "Well, my dear Isabel," says Aunt Luisa. She jabs the call button with the knob of her stick. "It is splendid to have seen you...so refreshing to be with the younger generation."

Beside them, the elevator rises clanking in its brass cage. "Dreadful apparatus," she remarks. "I cannot think why they have not simply got rid of it. A new, silent one. Modern..." The old head lifts imperiously, willing the listener to heed, and the Baronesa nods without speaking. The rattle of the elevator gate is loud in her ear.

El Dorado

"Why do you suppose it is," Mark said, "that the minute we hit the Quebec border, everything turned to lead? There were all those beautiful hills, and then bang, nothing but prairie. And now, these buildings..." He made a splayed-out gesture with his hand, flattening the buildings.

They were passing through what he took to be the main street of a little town. A pair of rival gas stations (why did they spell gas with a "z"?), a bar and a motel, both dwarfed by hulking neon signs, and then this row of unprosperous storefronts, each one painted a colour he associated with plastic. Where was the cool grace of the Vermont towns, the Greek-revival houses, the slim and modest steeples pointing into the sky?

Up ahead, a greystone Roman Catholic church and its accompanying greystone mansion swung into view. The church's towers, hugely top-heavy, appeared to be silver. "Will you look at that!" he said.

Beside him, Anne lifted her chin and gave him her serene and slightly severe smile. "All the towns up here are like this one," she said. "Just don't look."

Once out of the town he gunned the little Pontiac back to highway speed. Ninety, he calculated, was about fifty-five...at least he had the metric stuff under control. "By the way," he glanced over at her, "I'm pretty flush; I've been travelling all week, living on the company. You're sure you wouldn't like to stay at a hotel tonight?"

She shook her head. "It's because I haven't seen Perry for such an age. If we stayed in a hotel, she'd be hurt. She's the kind who likes to have people around, lots of noise..."

"Sounds relaxing." He spoke this time without turning his head. The highway had shrunk to a three-lane affair, the middle lane belonging equally, so far as he could tell, to cars travelling north or south. He had the uneasy sense that any one of these oncoming cars might, at any time, choose to leap across the white line.

Anne's voice was going on. "Last time I came up, she had this great big party. For me to meet people. I was feeling pretty terrible. It was just after Tyler moved out, and they were cheering me up. You remember…I told you?" He felt her glance at him, and he nodded. He'd heard a lot about Anne's former lover. Tyler had met and fallen wildly in love with a nineteen-year-old dancer, more or less in the space of half an hour. The following day, he'd moved across town to live with her, leaving behind a number of items, including most of his ties, and a new pair of tasselled Belgian loafers. The dancer had the kind of taste that ran to multi-coloured hair, pearlized eyeshadow and rhinestone studs in her fingernails. She'd had dozens of lovers and was further encumbered with a load of debts. Her declared ambition was to "make it big." The besotted Tyler could have no chance of hanging onto her. But even so she, Anne, did not want him back. The features of her delicate face hardened with distaste whenever such a possibility was mentioned. She looked, at these moments, as though she had just learned that her former love had acquired an unclean disease…which of course, thought Mark, he might well have.

"…She made hundreds of tiny meatballs in a special sauce and a huge chocolate mousse. Their little boy was just a baby…"

"I hate children," he offered, but didn't dare look to see how she was taking it. A truck, left-turn signal blinking furiously, was hurtling toward them down the ambiguous middle lane.

"He put his fist into the mousse, but he's three years old now, I think."

"The age of reason," he said. The truck was almost upon them.

"Well, I don't know," she said doubtfully. "She said he hasn't…" He missed the rest of her sentence. A massive wall of steel loomed above his window. The little Pontiac shuddered inside the roar.

"…Still likely to be rather chaotic," she was saying when the roar subsided.

"The traffic in this country is insane," he said accusingly.

"Dreadful," she agreed. "Perry says it's the French-Canadian mentality; they drive with their emotions, the way Europeans do. She thinks it's great. She's pregnant again... You'll like her husband, I'm pretty sure. He has a sweet accent."

"A sweet accent!" Ahead of them, a tractor lurched onto the highway. He lifted his foot from the accelerator. Spewing smoke, the tractor lumbered across all three lanes and pulled into the driveway of a small house.

"Not exactly an accent, more an intonation, I guess. He stresses different syllables; he calls her 'Peh-ree.'"

"How does he say Anne?" he asked.

"Anne," she said and then, as he turned to look at her, frowned. "I never get your jokes," she added, and he reflected, not for the first time, that this was true.

Several more towns swept past, each one fading swiftly into unplowed fields. From time to time he glanced over at Anne's small, straight nose and rounded chin. Her dark hair hung without a hint of curl to her jawline. The only way she could wear it, she'd confided, her hair was over-fine, it had no body.

They worked, he and she, for the same company. It was a little over four months since they'd met, at a sales promotion meeting. The meeting was one which she had helped to organize. Her department was Public Relations. His at the time was Systems Analysis. He'd been promoted since into Forward Planning.

At the meeting several people had asked if they were brother and sister. (More have asked since.) He himself had thought, gazing for the first time at the features so like his own, that if he wanted to marry, she was the sort of girl he should choose.

In the meantime, he had been assigned a business trip to Italy. The trip was scheduled for December. He proposed to add to it a week of skiing in the Dolomites. She'd already told him that she was fond of skiing. Travelling together would possibly constitute a good test of the relationship. Yet somehow, he had not yet got round to inviting her. He meant to. It was just he kept forgetting or he was unsure...about flight routes or snow conditions...something like that.

As they neared the big river, he could see the towers of Montreal rising on the far shore. The city meandered gracefully across two hills and then descended into the shoreline. One or two of the buildings shone a faint gold in the afternoon sun, and staring out across the water, he felt suddenly like an oldtime explorer, his mouth gone dry with discovery. A city here, so many miles to the north. It was like a promised land, a myth come true.

"I forget how far, but it's a dead-end," said Anne. They were following a street that sloped gradually upward through an aging residential section.

Driving with some care—twice he had to negotiate around street hockey games—he decided that the houses, most of them attached, must have stood here since the turn of the century; the rosy brick looked old, so did the gables and the elaborate stonework surrounding windows and doorways.

"The next block," said Anne. "You turn up there by the hedge."

The sign proclaimed it St. George's Place. The street was no more than half a block long. A semi-circle of brick houses rounded off the far end. The house Anne pointed out mirrored its neighbours...the same lead-paned windows and louvered shutters...except that these particular shutters, and the front door as well, had been painted a fiery orange.

"You must have a lot of trouble remembering which house," he said.

"Not really," said Anne in a distracted voice. She was collecting her purse and gloves.

As he turned off the engine, the orange-red front door opened, and a large female figure dressed in voluminous purple appeared in the doorway. "Götterdämmerung." The word lept into his mind. She looked as though she might burst into an aria. He flinched as the figure, nearly tripping, rushed down the steps. Not only was she extremely big, but she had quantities of lion-coloured hair. This hair flew behind her head in separate sections like thick cords. As she crossed the street toward the car, he realized that under the purple garment she was very pregnant.

The mother-to-be bounded around the hood of his car and pulled open Anne's door. Anne, laughing, was yanked from her seat. "You're huge..." Her voice trailing behind her as she disappeared through the open door sounded a trifle nervous. "You shouldn't be galloping like that...ouch! When is it due?"

"Not for eons...next month," he heard before he too got out of the car and then, while the two women were embracing, removed the suitcases from the trunk.

"You must meet Mark," came Anne's muffled voice. Her dark head had virtually disappeared into the tawny mass of hair. Freeing herself, she gestured toward Mark.

He stepped around the car to shake their hostess's hand and found himself looking into hazel eyes. Set deep in a wide, freckled face, the eyes gazed back at him with such directness that he nearly turned aside. Then she smiled, and he felt himself smile back. Everything about her suggested warmth...the dusty gold of her skin, her flushed cheeks, even the funny, flecked green-brown of her eyes. The lion species, he decided, letting go her hand, not his type.

She continued to stare at him. "Mark?" she repeated, as though his name came from an unknown language. "But you can't be." Her voice lilted girlishly. The three of them turned and crossed the street toward her house.

"My husband is Jean-Marc," she explained. "It's too confusing. Anne must have told you." They both glanced at Anne, who shook her head. "Don't you have a middle name, something else we can call you?" He stared at her. She kicked a child's toy truck off the sidewalk onto the grass before pointing at the brilliant door. "That's us," she said and turned again to Mark. "What about Kenneth? It's one of my favourite names."

"Kenneth?" he said.

"Good," said Perry. "Watch out for the stairs. The middle board is rotten."

After the brightness of the afternoon, the interior of the house seemed only half-lit. The entrance hall contained various objects which he gradually identified as a rattan chest, a small yellow tricycle, and an ironing board with two cantaloupe melons on it. Perry stopped. "You guys get the blue room at the back," she told them pointing upstairs. "Anne knows which one. It's not too gorgeous, but you won't hear Freddy at dawn, and that's worth a lot."

He and Anne were halfway up the stairs when the girlish voice stopped them. "Anne. Kenneth. Wait." Mark glanced back. She stood with her hands clasped together over her beach ball stomach. "Drinks," she called, "I almost forgot. You must be dying after all that driving. I'll get out the stuff. Do you still drink scotch, Anne?"

"Yes, but not a lot," said Anne. "You always pour me too much." She shifted her suitcase from one hand to the other.

"I haven't improved at all," Perry announced gazing happily up at them, "Except I'm not pouring much of anything these days. I throw up if I have more than three drinks."

"Wine doesn't bother me," she told them a few minutes later in the kitchen. "For now though, I'll just have a little scotch and a lot of water...ugh! Kenneth, you make the drinks. Glasses are beside the fridge." She slid a knife out of a rack above the stove and began to slice a bunch of celery stalks into thin strips.

"What a nice big kitchen," said Anne glancing around. "I'd forgotten."

"That's because last time you were here, half of it was the maid's room. From the olden days. We tore down the walls a year ago, just kept the pantry..." She pointed at a large closet that jutted into the room. "That's so I can close the door on some of the mess."

Mark nodded at the wisdom of this. He'd already noticed how, on the stairway and in the upstairs hall, toys lay in wait for them in every corner and how piles of folded laundry choked the big, old-fashioned bathroom. Here in the kitchen, preparations for dinner covered the counters. Long wooden spoons, bowls and cups, a mound of pastry on a board, little piles of sliced peppers and mushrooms and onions. One counter was smeared with the grey, gluey shells of shrimp.

"Oh, slime!" cried Perry, noticing the shells herself. Dropping her knife, she swiped at them, first with her hand and then with a paper towel. The latter proved more effective. "There," she said stepping back from the counter and dumping the towelful of debris into the garbage. Shrimp shells stuck to her arm; another had hooked onto a seam of her purple poncho.

"Hold on," said Mark. He picked the shells off her one by one.

Perry stood still for this operation. "Oh, I know," she told them, "I need a keeper."

"Probably," said Mark.

"Oh, but really, she does things very well," protested Anne. "You do, Perry. You're very organized in your way."

"He's just being funny," said Perry. "But you're right, Annie. You're always on my side. And of course I am very self-sufficient really. Here. Grab that basket of crackers. Let's go sit with our drinks."

The living room had the look of a well-worn library. Several corduroy-covered armchairs and a sagging leather sofa formed a horseshoe around the fireplace. A faded Bokara rug covered the floor. Its pattern of medallions suggested that it might once have been red and black, though the colours now were as muted and varied as the rows of books that crammed the shelves on either side of the fireplace.

Perry put her drink down and collapsed onto the sofa. "Veins," she explained, propping her legs on the coffee table and pulling up a corner of the purple poncho to reveal an elastic bandage wrapped around one calf.

"Awful," said Anne. Her nose wrinkled with sympathy and something like disbelief...as if she couldn't imagine such a condition, either for herself or for her friend.

"You're telling me," said Perry. "It feels like being old."

Mark had retreated to one of the corduroy chairs. Encased in it he sat nursing his drink, watching and listening to the two women. Anne, sedate Anne, with this off-the-wall female. They'd gone to the same college, he knew, and they'd travelled together more than once. It was during a trip to Paris that Perry had met her husband, the as yet unseen Jean-Marc. Beyond those facts, Anne had come forth with very little. Mark watched her now as she threw back her head and laughed. Her cheeks had flushed up, and, in spite of the fact that she seldom smoked, she'd taken a pack of cigarettes from her purse and was offering one to Perry.

"Ciggies!" cried Perry as though spotting an old friend. "You knew. I haven't seen one of those for years."

"They must smoke something up here?" said Mark.

"Canadian brands," said Perry. "They're better packed of course, but it's not the same." She grinned at Anne. "Remember those garbage sticks we smoked in Greece...Papastratos? When we finally got hold of some Marlboros, they tasted like heaven."

"Have one." Anne extended the pack again, but Perry had extinguished her initial look of anticipation.

"I can't," she said. "Not when I'm preggers."

"Oh, right," said Anne. "Bad for the baby."

Perry nodded. "But the next time you come," she promised, as if she'd somehow failed to be entertaining.

For the next ten minutes she and Anne talked about trips they had taken. "Do you remember?" Perry cried at various intervals, "...the pie throwing contest in Menlo Park?" "...the night all those German students took us to the Plaka?" "...that man in Florence who fell in love with us?"

Anne smiled indulgently. "It was you," she said, "...you the man fell in love with."

Perry laughed. "Oh, it was both of us. He just couldn't believe how big I was." She turned to Mark. "In Europe, Kenneth, I was a capital-G giant. The notes that man wrote! He left them on the car...all over the city. Wherever we parked, we'd come back and find these terrible, mushy notes. It was hysterical!" She swallowed the rest of her scotch. "We wrote notes back. Crazy things. We were awful." She said this happily, wiping her mouth with a graceful slash of her long hand.

"You must have been," he said. Her excited face seemed exalted.

Nodding she pushed back her ropes of hair. "You guys should have another drink, you know. Jean-Marc is playing squash. He has a regular Saturday game. He won't get home for at least half an hour, and I have to collect Freddy from his nap or he'll stay awake all night." She pulled herself sideways from the deep sofa and got up. A forgotten cracker slid down the side of her stomach and dropped onto the rug.

Awakened and fed, Freddy was brought in to meet Anne and Mark. Gone were the giggles and cries that had reached them from the direction of the kitchen. Freddy entered the living room in silence. Slight and dark, staring from one to the other guest, he managed to walk almost entirely within the folds of the purple poncho. When Perry sat down, he laid his head on her knee. She stroked his shiny, child's hair—the jet strands floated between her fingers—and spoke quietly to him. After a moment, he climbed up beside her on the sofa and then, from the evident safety of this vantage point, offered a smile and a soft hello to the guests.

"That's nicer," Perry told him. "People get sad if you don't talk to them." She fished a flat red book out from under a magazine and flipped it open. "Don't mind me," she told Anne and Mark. "This is Freddy's storytime. It's better now than later, in the middle of dinner. Right, Freddy?" Freddy nodded. He was sitting up straight, preparing to attend the reading. Perry began in her light, trusting voice, "'Joey Beaver had been diving in the lake all afternoon. He was looking for his best stick...'"

The story, a saga of two beavers, had ended, and Mark had made fresh drinks all around when the front door clicked and then banged.

"Daddy?" asked Freddy and, at Perry's nod, climbed down off the sofa. He raced from the room crying, "Papa, Papa!"

A minute later, he made a triumphal re-entry aloft in his father's arms. The source of Freddy's slender darkness was now apparent. Side by side, the two faces gazed down on the guests...the same sweet smiles, the same brown, lash-fringed eyes.

"So. You have arrived. It is a pleasure for us." Jean-Marc's enunciation was precise and, as Anne had implied, only mildly accented. Setting Freddy down, he bent to kiss his wife. He did this on both her cheeks, pausing to whisper in her ear.

He spent almost as long kissing Anne. Her cheeks reddened, but she did not, to Mark's surprise, look affronted. Nor did she pull away immediately from the hand Jean-Marc laid on her shoulder. "It is too long since you have been in Montreal," he told her solemnly.

"A couple of years...Freddy was just walking." She glanced over at Mark and lifted a tentative hand as though to begin introductions.

Perry's voice sang out from the sofa, "This is Kenneth...no, not Kenneth..."

Smiling faintly, Anne leaned back in her chair. Mark rose to his feet. Jean-Marc glanced toward his wife and then stepped forward offering his hand. "My wife is an eccentric woman. No doubt you have already noticed this." His grip was surprisingly strong.

"Jean-Marc's just being contentious," said Perry. "Don't listen to him. "But she turned toward her husband with attentive eyes.

He smiled as he sat down. "You confuse people," he told her.

Jean-Marc, it seemed evident, was confused about nothing. Corporate litigation, he explained to Mark, was his specialty. Singled out as a protégé by one of the senior partners in his firm, he travelled often with this man. From these trips he had fashioned a series of funny and self-deprecating anecdotes. His duties, it seemed, had not always concerned questions of the law. "All the same, I have been very lucky," he told Mark. "Too many trips..." He shrugged. "But New York, Hong Kong, Paris, Milan. This is not so bad?" The smile he gave Mark was amused and conspiratorial...as if they, the men, were the more knowledgeable, more cynical species.

His English was fluent; he never paused to search for a word, never substituted a French term for an English one. In fact, French seemed to be spoken in the house only between Jean-Marc and his little boy, whom he called Fredéric. For his part Freddy/Fredéric alternated without hesitation between the two languages. Perry seemed to know always what they were saying, but she spoke only in English. Hearing the sentences fly between father and son—was French actually spoken faster than English?—Mark felt his own tongue thick in his mouth. How inept, it suddenly seemed, to speak only one language.

While Jean-Marc was recounting one of his stories, this about a client with two mistresses, Perry departed for the kitchen. She reappeared after about a quarter of an hour and, leaning against the door frame, demanded help. A sheen of sweat overlay her flushed skin.

"No, not you." She held out a hand as Anne made a move to rise. "I need muscle, not expertise. We're almost ready, but I need some carrying. Kenneth, could you?"

It was only after he'd risen and was following her to the kitchen—striding, with straight loose hips, she hardly looked pregnant from the back—that Mark realized there had never been, not even for an instant, a question of Jean-Marc being the one to help his wife.

"I drop things," declared Perry over her shoulder as she banged open the kitchen door.

He followed her into the steaming kitchen. A long, green noodle was plastered to a cabinet door above the stove. Several pots fumed on the stove. Perry instructed him to pour the boiling contents of the largest one into a colander in the sink. "Tagliatelle," she said. "With all the water it's so heavy I'm afraid to lift it." She glanced down at her stomach as though it had inexplicably appeared there. "Watch out for the steam," she warned now as he tipped up the big pot. "It doesn't look dangerous, but it can burn you."

In a smaller pot something like cream sauce bubbled lightly. "Shrimps and scallops," she informed him. "With a julienne of veggies...in a cream and pernod sauce. Fabulous. You'll love it." He smiled and then swallowed. Something, the smell or her ecstatic description of her own cooking, had made his mouth water.

"I invented it," she told them proudly at dinner. Mark watched Anne picking the scallops one by one out of her serving. Perry was still explaining. "...I did all the shopping at the Atwater Market...that's a place sort of like Faneuil Hall. We have wonderful markets here, especially in the fall..."

Mark had a sudden vision of her bigger-than-lifesize figure striding through the crowded stalls, a market basket over one arm (though he knew this was fanciful), arguing cheerfully with the vendors, fingering vegetables, sniffing into barrels of apples. A smile swept her face whenever something she found pleased her.

It was exactly his idea of a wife. The knowledge shot through him like a sudden fever. A big, golden wife. It was a vision which he knew would have infuriated every woman of his acquaintance...including Anne and, no doubt, Perry herself.

At the moment the object of his fantasy was laughing loudly. "It's a matter of greed," she cried and waved her fork. She did this practically every time she spoke. "I always want everything in sight...all I can think of is how hungry I am..."

In the next minute she was on her feet, again waving the fork. "The salad. Annie, you stay and talk with the prince." She pronounced "prince" in the French way.

"You don't want me to help?" Anne asked.

Perry shook her head and pointed the fork at Jean-Marc. "The prince wouldn't have a woman to charm." She collected their plates and headed into the kitchen. They could hear the pile of plates bang onto the counter as the door swung shut behind her.

Jean-Marc smiled his sweet smile at Anne and then at Mark, who was getting to his feet. "Ah, you Americans," he said tolerantly and reached for the wine.

In the kitchen Mark found Perry standing on a stool in the pantry. The purple poncho swirled around her ankles. One ragged end of the elastic bandage hung below the hem. "You shouldn't do that," he told her. She peered down at him through the ropes of her hair, and he thought that his admonition had sounded fussy. "I mean," he explained, "you're not supposed to fall, are you? It's not..."

"Oh, but I have very good balance," she assured him. "I teach aerobic dancing. Here. Take this, will you?" She handed down a small bottle of wine. As he took it from her and turned to put it on a lower shelf, folds of the poncho brushed his face. "It's Hungarian Tokay," she told him. "Someone gave it to us. I just remembered it." The stool wobbled as she shifted her feet.

"Listen," he said again. "Come on down, will you?" He reached up. "Come on..." She bent over then and put her hands on his shoulders, submitting to be lifted down. The sudden weight of her was terrific; his knees nearly buckled. As she dropped, they staggered sideways into the door frame, and then she was standing, eye to eye with him, laughing into his face. He kept his hands under her arms, holding her in the pantry. What he wanted to do now—and it seemed like the plan of a lifetime—was to kiss her wide mouth. But something, a scruple or a scrap of fear, held him back. Instead, with the same deliberate motion he'd watched Jean-Marc use, Mark kissed each of her cheeks as if blessing her.

The moment was long and cushioned in silence. She stood motionless, and he felt, as he had when he was picking shrimp shells off her arm, that he was fixing her. He was blotting with his lips the freckles sprinkled over her skin. As he straightened his head, she gave him a pleased, lazy smile. Her long eyes slid closed, then slowly opened. "Did you fall in love with me already?" she asked without moving from his embrace.

He said nothing. She had leapt, in a single, probably half-meant sentence, more barriers than he'd managed in a lifetime.

"Listen," she went on, "...men do...if they can stand my size. But don't worry. It doesn't last." She laughed, and then as he stared at her face—they were standing so close to one another he could almost breathe her in—the triumph melted from her eyes. She tilted her head in the direction of the dining room. "It really doesn't," she said and immediately shook her head, as if forbidding him to respond. Her hair swung back and forth with the momentum. "He was so beautiful when I married him," she confided. Mark could feel her whisper against his face. "You never saw such a pretty man." Her smile was returning. "He's half French too. Did you know? I mean French from France. He has all these relatives in the Loire Valley. I thought it was too exotic for words. I still do sometimes, but it does wear a little thin..." She laughed again. "You're just about the screaming opposite from him, aren't you? You never hang out too far, right? You never just go and...do something?"

"That sounds like 'the screaming opposite' of you," he suggested and heard the note of challenge in his own voice. She still had not stepped back, nor had he released his hold on her, and now he imagined that the warmth from her stomach and her hormone-swollen breasts was spreading up through his brain, banishing some hereditary chill. "Someday..." he promised, surprising himself even more.

She smiled now and, lifting her long hands, placed them against his shoulders. "Come on, Kenneth," she said and gave him a backward push. "Salad time."

Stepping back into the dining room, Mark was grateful for the big wooden bowl of salad he'd been assigned to bring to the table. He carried it like an explanation offered. "Perry's still grating something," he said. The other two glanced up at him, but neither gave him the fishy stare he felt he deserved. "She's coming in a minute," he added.

Anne blinked at him. "We don't have any plates."

"Perry said she'd bring them. I've been ordered to sit down." He set the bowl down in front of Perry's empty place and returned to his own chair.

"So," said Jean-Marc turning to him. "Anne tells me she organized the conference at which you met." He smiled encouragingly at Mark, as if the story of their meeting ought to have special appeal.

Mark nodded. "That's right," he said heartily. "She did. It's her department."

"Well," Anne said, looking pleased. "There were other people too. I wasn't the only one putting it together. It was just that there were extra..." She stopped, pursing her lips slightly, as the dining room door swung open. The figure of Perry appeared framed in the widening rectangle of fluorescent light. One of her hands clutched several plates. The other she held aloft, clenched into a fist.

"Watch out, everybody!" she cried, plunging into the room. "I've grated my knuckles into the carrots." She handed the plates to Mark and then, stepping around Anne's chair, opened her fist over the salad bowl. A wad of something orange dropped onto the lettuce. "Cannibal salad," she announced into the silence and plunked down onto her chair.

Jean-Marc laughed. "My little gourmet wife," he said raising his wine glass to her. She made a face down the table at him and then smiled. Watching them look at one another, Mark felt a sudden release within himself. In this house, with this couple... The thought escaped him uncompleted, but the little twisting of guilt in his stomach had eased, and he settled back in his chair.

Perry glanced around at Anne and then at Mark. "Don't mind me," she told them. "It's only carrots...for colour. Just mix it around when you serve yourself. Did I miss anything important while I was out there?" She sucked loudly at the knuckles of two of her fingers.

Anne shook her head. "You didn't miss anything," she told her friend, and her expression was both fond and exasperated. "Nothing happens when you're not there."

As the salad and then the cheese and dessert courses progressed, Mark was aware of himself growing more and more heady. The encounter in the kitchen had left him warm and excited, and though he couldn't resist staring at Perry's big face gleaming in the wash of candle light, the feeling was more comprehensive. It was as if the combination of her and of being called by another name and the parade of delicious food and Jean-Marc's whimsical cynicism and the still hopeful, though far-off cries of the dark-haired little boy who, after riding a final time through the dining room on the yellow tricycle, had been borne away to bed—as if all this were the furniture and fixtures of another world to which he, Mark, had been transported in an unexpected flash of colliding realities. Matter and anti-matter. And something, though he couldn't put his finger on what, had been annihilated in the flash.

He awoke the next morning in halting steps. After backsliding twice into a kind of drugged sleep, he was induced finally by the strong light coming in from the window to abandon a dream in which he was watching Perry ride an oversize tricycle down St. George's Place. As she headed into the traffic of the cross street, he tried to call out a warning. But his voice produced no volume; his cry came out a thin, nearly soundless wail. She turned and waved gaily to him. At this point he noticed a large truck looming ahead of her, and then... But already he'd lost it. The light from the window had won out. He rolled over onto his back and, without opening his eyes, pulled the duvet up to his nose. He could smell a faint, dusty odour, something like bath powder. The end of the previous evening began to emerge from his memory. He recalled the splintering crash of a big crystal bowl filled with something fluffy and yellow, the intense, smoky sweetness of the Tokay, cigar smoke... And hadn't there been a fiery dose of Armagnac as well? No legal substance, in fact, seemed to have been left untried. Somewhere along the line someone must have done some cleaning up, though he wasn't sure who. He did remember climbing the stairs, stepping around the toys, the coolness of the guest bedroom, and recalled with a start of embarrassment that he'd gone to sleep without laying a hand on Anne. He couldn't, in fact, remember having said anything whatsoever to Anne the previous night. Lying in bed with the duvet guarding half his face, he felt suddenly uneasy. But couldn't he just say he'd been drunk? Probably she already knew that. Probably she thought he was lucky to have got out of his clothes and into bed. The guest room, he noticed now, was very cold. His head hurt in two places. He was extremely thirsty. His lips and tongue felt cemented together. He made a sound that resembled the syllable "Anne." There was no answer. "Anne," he croaked again. Silence. Tentatively he opened one eye, closed it and opened the other. The bed across from his was empty. He opened both eyes. His watch, which he was still wearing, told him it was nearly eleven o'clock. Anne, who tended to be brisk in the morning, had undoubtedly already risen. He swung his feet out of bed and sat up. Pain rolled across his forehead.

In the bathroom he found a plastic glass—yellow, with "Freddy" painted across it in scarlet nail polish—and drank down two glassfuls of water. He was considering what to do next when the door opened and Freddy/Fredéric himself appeared in the doorway. His puppy eyes stared up at Mark with evident interest. It was clear he didn't intend to leave.

"Bonjour," offered Mark. He made himself smile.

Freddy didn't smile back but did say, "Bonjour." This greeting was followed by a sentence in French which began with "Maman..."

Mark stared down at him for a moment and then realized his fundamental error. "I'm sorry, Freddy," he said, trying not to exhale in the direction of the small face. "I don't speak French like you...only English."

Freddy began again. "Mommy say...Mommy say brepfes ready. But..." He shook his head, still solemnly gazing up at Mark. "You don' haf to if you are frowing up."

"I don't have to eat if I'm throwing up?" asked Mark. Freddy shook his head again, presumably in affirmation.

"Pancakes," he said informatively after a short pause. Then he turned and ran toward the stairs.

Coming downstairs a few moments later, Mark wondered how he could ever have thought the interior of the house dim. A brash morning light bounced off sections of floor and wall. The windows glinted threateningly. He ducked his head and tried to veil his eyes. Part of the dining room floor, he noticed as he passed through, was streaked with a pale yellow substance. In the kitchen he was greeted with a certain amount of amusement.

"I have some aspirin in my bag," Anne told him. "You must need a few."

He nodded. "Thanks. I already took three. How did you guess?"

"That you'd need them?" said Anne. "Well, you seemed a little odd last night..."

"Odd?" repeated Mark.

"Drunk," said Perry. "She means drunk, don't you, Annie? It was Jean-Marc's lethal Armagnac. It's done in all kinds of guests."

Jean-Marc, who had been stirring and mixing something at one of the counters, turned now and flashed one of his beautiful, sympathetic smiles. "There is no sense to be brave," he said holding out a tumbler full of Bloody Mary.

"Take it," said Perry. "You'll feel more human." She was buttering a pancake for Freddy, who was perched on a high stool at the other end of the counter.

"Do you want a pancake?" she asked after a minute. "I'm making another batch. It's my own recipe...whole wheat flour and..." She stopped at the sight of his grimace.

"Thank you," he told her. "I'm sure you mean well." She laughed, and he felt again a kinship between them. Whatever had happened last night must have risen from some kind of inevitability. A need in himself. And maybe in her too. Indeed, wasn't there something husbandless about her now as she moved about the kitchen pouring cups of coffee for each of them, something vulnerable and even helpless? And yet why should he think this? He moved to a corner to get out of the way of her activities. And why should he think, as he did, that in embracing her in the middle of her kitchen he'd been offering her some sort of support? Anne moved over to his side, and dutifully, feeling like a hypocrite of the first order, he draped his arm over her shoulders.

Jean-Marc held up the new pitcher of Bloody Marys which he'd been preparing. "Top you up, Anne?"

She shook her head. In the curve of Mark's arm, her shoulders felt frail. "One's enough," she said.

Jean-Marc shook his head. "But that is never true," he told her cheerfully.

"Freddy want more syrup," Freddy announced to his mother. "S'il t'plaît," he added as his father glanced at him.

Jean-Marc set the pitcher down on the counter. His labour done, he pivoted and leaned gracefully against the refrigerator. He was already shaved, and with his drink in one hand and attired in a wine velvet dressing gown, he looked like an ad for some expensive brand of aftershave.

He gazed around now with eyes as clear and untroubled as if there had been no scotch, no bottles of wine, no Armagnac... Mark took a large swallow of Bloody Mary. "You Canadians are remarkable," he told Jean-Marc. "I feel as if I spent the night with my head in a bottle."

"It is our training." Jean-Marc gave him one of the smiles. "For the cold, you see. We must drink."

"That's what he tells me," said Perry. She had syrup dripping from the sleeve of her bathrobe. "It's probably true, actually. Winter goes on forever here." As she swung around to grab her cup of coffee, a fine thread of syrup ran down her hand. "Oh, shit," she said mildly. "Toss me that dish cloth, will you, Annie?" And Mark suddenly knew why she seemed husbandless. It was Jean-Marc's effortless perfection—his boy's face (what had Perry called him, a "pretty man?") his self-contained, untouchable charm, his ease with every aspect of the weekend and indeed of his life—that made him seem unmarried. He had none of the distracted concern Mark had noted in his other married friends and especially in those with children. No wonder Perry seemed unmarried. There was no one here who acted like her husband.

Some hours later he stood with Anne on a downtown sidewalk. They were both gazing up at Perry, who was poised, hair blowing wildly, on the topmost step of a fifty-foot wide cement stairway. Behind her rose the edifice that housed the Musée des Beaux Arts. It resembled, Mark had already decided, an immense tomb, hung in this case with banners advertising the presence of Picasso's works within. The wind slapped these banners to and fro so that their message took some time to decipher.

Perry cupped her hands around her mouth. "It's all going to be worth it. All, all..." Anne and Mark could barely understand her. "Jean-Marc...just parking," she yelled as they mounted the first tier of steps.

A baby sitter had arrived after the lengthy breakfast, and the two couples had driven downtown in separate cars so that Anne and Mark could leave directly for home from the museum. Mark had decided he didn't want to face that schizophrenic, three-lane highway at dusk.

"We're coming," Anne called up. She sounded weary climbing the long flight of steps and also as though she hoped Perry would not scream at them again. During the ten minute drive downtown—and all through brunch, now that he thought of it—she had barely spoken. That brief warming that she'd seemed to experience in Perry's company yesterday, and in Jean-Marc's company too, didn't seem evident today. Was it just his getting drunk and passing out that had cooled her, or did she somehow sense the connection made between him and Perry? Not that it was so much of a connection. Five minutes outside of reality...or in another reality. But still he felt chagrined and, now as the day wore on, somewhat surprised at himself as well. What had got into him? Aside from the major practicalities—Perry being both married and vastly pregnant—Anne was so much more his type.

Solicitously he took her arm and glanced sideways at the thin curtain of her hair. "Museums like this one always want to exhaust you before you begin," he told her. "You're supposed to be fagged out by the time you reach the door so you'll appreciate the uplift of art."

"Picasso's not exactly an uplifting kind of artist," she said seriously.

As they neared the top of the steps, Perry was making circular, hurry-up motions with her hands. "It's just about our time," she announced. "Jean-Marc had better get here soon." The wind caught the man's tweed coat she was wearing and blew it open. Her stomach emerged momentarily, like a big kettle ineptly concealed beneath today's tentlike costume, which was red. In the same blast, her hair swept back, and she flung her hands up to the sides of her face as though her whole life were about to blow away. To Mark, gazing up at her, she looked heroic. A Viking queen. He could imagine her standing like this, on the summit of some mountain or temple, staring out toward the great northern river and wondering when, if ever, her warriors would return.

"What?" he said to Anne. He was aware vaguely of her having spoken.

"I said, the crowd doesn't look too bad," she repeated stoically.

"No," he agreed. "Not too bad." There were perhaps two dozen people standing around on the upper steps. Most of them had been intermittently staring at Perry since her first shriek.

Jean-Marc, his overcoat slung over his shoulders like a cape, came dashing up the stairs behind them now. A cigar protruded from his mouth. He removed it just ahead of Perry's wild grab. "So," he said fending her off. "Now, now, my dear... So, you are ready for Picasso." He produced the tickets from his breast pocket. These had been purchased ahead of time. A secretary in his office, he'd assured them, his smile illuminating his face, had been glad to run the errand for him.

"This exhibition is a very fine one," he told Mark. "It is lucky to have it in Montreal. We have a new director of the museum who is a friend of Jacqueline Picasso." This is how things are done, he implied, and you and I of course know this. He stubbed out the cigar in a brass ashtray stand just inside the great doorway. "Chez Picasso," he announced cheerfully as they entered. His arm swept in a wide arc as though all that they perceived about them at this moment—marble columns, more flights of stairs, even the babble of echoing voices—were his personal offering.

For nearly half an hour he led them from room to room, once in a while telling them something about a particular period. It was evident the paintings fascinated him and that he'd studied them. "It's more fun with Jean-Marc, isn't it?" said Perry as they stood gazing at a painting of two musicians. And Mark had to agree. He had his eyes so often on his host's face, in fact, that he caught the sudden frown that flickered over the boyish features. Turning, Mark saw a young, dark-haired woman emerge with purposeful step from the crowd at the nearest doorway.

"Eh, Jean-Marc!" Her voice pierced their foursome. Its owner wore a tight, shiny skirt, possibly leather, and heels so high Mark wondered how she could walk without tottering. But walk she did, straight toward Jean-Marc, as if she meant to march right into him. Jean-Marc's eyes narrowed into a squint for a second before the habitual sweet smile opened his face. The girl stopped a foot from him and laid her gloved hands on his forearms.

"So, Jean-Marc." She spoke in a parody of tenderness, looking up into his face. Her next sentences were in rapid French. The only words Mark caught came at the end—"...jolie femme"—spoken just before she spun around and thrust her hand at Perry. "So, Mrs. de Beaufort. Pleased to meet you." She grabbed Perry's hand and shook it hard but gingerly, like someone shaking down a thermometer. There was at least a head's difference between the two, the smaller woman a sleek, burrowing animal to Perry's lion. Mark glanced briefly over at Anne. An expression of distaste, the one he knew well, had hardened like a glaze on her features.

"You're from Jean-Marc's office?" Perry was asking. She smiled down at the girl.

"That's right," said the girl. "When Jean Marc send his girl for the tickets, I just ask her, get me one too." Dropping Perry's hand she cast a quick look, which Mark took to be defiant, in Jean-Marc's direction.

"It's a wonderful show, isn't it?" said Perry, but the girl had already turned back to Jean-Marc.

"I think I meet your friends too," she said to Jean-Marc.

"You did?" he asked, clearly amazed.

"I think I meet them now," the girl said. She turned and took Mark's hand. At the same time as his hand was being shaken, he was treated to a brief, measuring look. Anne got the same handshake a few seconds later but no look. "Pleased to meet you," the girl said to them and then tapped herself on the pendant that hung almost between her breasts. "Solange Drouin," she stated.

Jean-Marc pronounced Anne's name and then Mark's. "They are from Boston," he added, as if this fact would preclude further discussion. To Mark he said gravely, "Solange is a lawyer from my office." His eyes, restored to imperturbability, rested for a second on Mark's face, and then, to Mark's astonishment, one beautiful, fringed eye closed and reopened in an unmistakable wink.

"Pleased to meet you, pleased to meet you," mimicked Perry. They'd left Solange in the exhibition rooms upstairs and were standing near the checkroom door while Jean-Marc procured their coats. Perry stamped from Mark to Anne, shaking their hands with the same vigorous yank the girl Solange had used. "I think I meet you now."

Jean-Marc stepped around her trying to hand out their coats. "You are a silly woman," he told her. "Stop this."

But Perry laid her hands on his forearms. "Eh, Jean-Marc," she said in a fake accent and then added in her own voice, "Those girls take you seriously, you know."

"Solange is like that with every man in the office, my dear," said Jean-Marc. "It's not me especially."

"It's you," said Perry. She turned to thrust her arms into the sleeves of the giant tweed coat which Jean-Marc held open for her. Over her head now as she struggled, her husband caught Mark's eye and again pulled a humorous face...man to man. And Mark felt himself smile back.

"I expect she wanted to get a look at me," said Perry a moment later. They were walking across the foyer toward the great door. "Jean-Marc's a terrific flirt. Listen, Annie, don't take three years to come back this time. As soon as I've finished up with business," she patted her stomach, "we'll have some fun."

Anne smiled. "Good luck with the baby," she said as Jean-Marc pushed open the heavy door.

"Don't remind me!" said Perry. "Lousy old childbirth. It's a rotten way to spend a day." She clutched the huge tweed coat to her chest as the wind leapt at them. Mark thought suddenly that he had never seen a coat so hideous. He wanted to snatch it off her. "Last time I screamed the place down. My mother was disgusted with me. She came all the way from Minneapolis, and then she was disgusted with me. She thought I must be the Italian girl in the next caseroom. She was horrified when she found out all the noise was me. I mean, the poor Italian girl was nice and quiet. It was all me." Perry laughed, but her eyes blinked rapidly as though something hurt her still. "I couldn't believe no one had ever told me how much it would hurt." Gazing down at Anne, she looked puzzled and, except for a slight bunching at the corners of her mouth and eyes, very young.

"Well," said Anne in her practical way, "Probably this time it'll be easier. You know...second time and all. Just don't think about it."

At the foot of the cement stairs, the couples turned to face each other. Their cars were parked in opposite directions. Blades of wind slashed between them. Flaps of their own clothing enveloped their various embraces. The two women hugged first while the men shook hands. Then, as Jean-Marc was placing his kisses on Anne's cheeks, Mark wrapped his arms around Perry.

"Thanks for the great dinner...and everything," he said into the lashing ropes of hair.

She leaned back and looked into his eyes. Her smile, he thought, was fond...and knowing too, as though he and she were old collaborators. "You're welcome, Kenneth," she told him. "Come again." The hard ball of her stomach pressed companionably against him.

For another moment he kept his arm around her shoulders. His fingers dug into the rough tweed...as if he were fortifying her in some way, making up for the smile he had given her husband. When she turned her head to say something across him to Anne, her heavy hair swept like an acknowledgement over his cheek and jaw. On his other side, Anne lifted her gentle chin and smiled at whatever was being said, and Mark, even as he admired once again the classical balance and clarity of her features, knew that he would go to Italy alone.

"I always miss her," said Anne. "Him too. After I've been with them." She brushed back her hair, and Mark, glancing sideways, saw that her expression was bleak.

He nodded and shifted his hands on the wheel. He had been thinking just now that the interior of the car seemed cavernous, the two of them shrunk to the size of children. "They're quite the characters," he said.

"That's what everyone always said about her," said Anne. "She did the wildest things. You liked her, didn't you?" Her voice was not accusing.

"I liked her," said Mark. He pulled out to pass a car full of women. The middle one in the back seat wore a nun's headdress. "This is a much better road," he added. They had, after a last minute consultation with the map, chosen a different highway, a route that proceeded more or less straight east but promised, in due course, to intersect with another highway, also of the four-lane variety, which would then take them south to the border. Sweeping around the slower car, Mark decided to gun the car a bit...a last hour of speed before the border. The highway had emptied of traffic around the same time as prairie had given way to a pleasant series of hills. A few of these, in the far distance, appeared grand enough to be deemed mountains. "I liked him too," he added. "I even liked the little kid. He spoke such terrific French." He turned to smile at her and saw that her cheek was wet and the end of her nose had turned pink. She was fumbling in her purse. "Anne?" he said. "Anne...what's wrong?"

"Nothing..." She produced a kleenex and began to wipe her eyes.

"Come on." He reached over and laid his hand on her thigh. Guilt congealed in his stomach. Did she understand the extent of his infatuation, how warm and bedazzled he'd been feeling since the windswept goodbye at the foot of the Musée des Beaux Arts?

She shook her head unhappily. "I always feel this way after I leave Perry...always. I feel like something's missing."

"Because she's so super-alive?" he said.

"Because...yes...I guess that's right. It's hard to explain. I mean, I know the house is a mess and everything's wild, but they're so..." She shook her head again. "You felt it too, didn't you?"

"Yes," he said. "I felt it too."

Ahead of them a green highway sign announced the approach of some place called Ste-Justine-du-Lac. "There's a town coming, I think," he said. "Want to stop for a hamburger or something? Coffee?" Taking her muffled and monosyllabic reply for an affirmative, he signalled a right turn.

The restaurant featured a single plate-glass window and a shiny red roof. It looked like any diner except that, above the front edge of the roof, towered an unlit neon sign. At night the large script letters must flood the parking area with light… "Auberge du Lac" pouring over its customers. Mark pronounced the words in his mind as he slowed the car and glanced around. In fact, he'd spotted no hint of shoreline, no glimmer of water. But, still, there must be a lake somewhere around…closer to town maybe. On the other side of the road, directly opposite the diner, stood a gas station. Another neon sign, this one hanging above the pumps, advertised "Libre Service." Mark wondered if this meant no tipping but decided not to tax Anne with the question. Her lips were still puffy though she was now studiously applying lipstick.

He pulled onto the apron of gravel that surrounded the diner, then eased the Pontiac in between two cars that resembled, in model and year, the cars of his high school days. One was an old Cadillac convertible, rusted and impossibly long, its savage fins jutting out beyond the other cars. He had a sudden of vision of Perry at the wheel of such a car, surrounded by friends big and blond as herself, all of them laughing and screaming along some leafy, sunlit country road, their hair flying behind them in a great tangled web of gold.

"Could you just bring me out a Coke or something? I feel silly making us take the time to go in and find a table and everything…" Anne's voice startled him. He glanced round at her and realized he had been fumbling for a considerable number of seconds with the buckle of his seat belt. The pink had receded from her nose and lips.

Unbuckling the belt, he reached over and pushed back the fragile wings of her hair. Then he pulled her toward him and kissed her, first on each damp cheek and then on her newly lipsticked mouth. He could feel the stickiness, taste the greasy perfume, and the intimacy, the discount-drugstore, shopping-mall ordinariness of it, was like being inside her closet or opening her bathroom cabinet.

When he released her, she bowed her head and rested her forehead on his shoulder. Her hair floated against his lips and stuck. "Listen," he said, rubbing off the hairs with his fingers, "It's okay. We can go in and have whatever you want. Coffee. Food. Anything. We have time." She nodded into his shoulder.

Watching her get out of the car a few moments later, he felt both doomed and oddly triumphant, as though he had in some way grown larger. "Why don't we find a decent motel and spend the night in this town?" he said suddenly. The gravel crunched under their feet. Anne, stopping to pick some out of her shoe, stared up at him. "There must be a good restaurant over on the lake. We can have dinner...no Armagnac...and get up early..."

"We'd have to get up in the middle of the night." She was still staring at him. "Maybe no one in the town speaks English." He said nothing. "Well..." her face was changing, "Well, I guess we'd manage." She was trying, he guessed, to produce a carefree expression. He thought of this as he pulled open the door to the diner and was greeted with the smell of French fries. He thought too of how he would click off the lamp that night, in the as yet unlocated motel, and take her in his arms...of how, in the dark, he would imagine himself in the dangerous embrace of the she-lion...the Viking queen...his mythical golden wife.

As they entered, the overheated air closed round them... rich not only with the heat and grease of French fries, but with the throatier aromas of cigarette smoke and beer and coffee. A drum-enhanced chant throbbed forth from the juke box in the corner. But it was the live voices that grabbed him. They rose from the row of customers seated along the wooden counter and from various booths and tables scattered throughout the room. An amiable clash of gossip and opinion, no doubt, but none of them—he was almost certain of this—not a single, busy, excited one of these voices was speaking in his language.

He would look a fool, trying to order. And how would he know what anyone said to them? His curdled, phrasebook French was not up to the task. Beside him Anne stood motionless. "You were right about the language business," he told her. "Absolutely right."

He had already turned toward the door, when the tug on his arm halted him. "Let's sit over there." She let go his sleeve and pointed toward an empty table. "Over there by the window."

He followed her, working his way gingerly through the tables. As they were sitting down, she glanced at him. "It's a funny feeling. Not understanding a word anyone's saying." He nodded. Her delicate hands extracted a paper napkin from the holder and began wiping her fingertips one by one. "I feel much better though," she added, and he saw that she was smiling at him, almost as though she were trying to reassure him. "Could I have a grilled cheese?" she asked now. "And coffee?"

"Sure," he said. "They must have stuff like that. Go crazy." He reached for the pair of menus jammed between the napkin holder and the plastic ketchup bottle. Perhaps from the menu he could figure out what to say. Or maybe Anne would know.

"Don't you suppose this is good for us?" Anne's voice was gentle. "Something to shake us up, or something like that?"

Handing her a menu, he stared at her features. This was how she would look when she was old...too earnest, a little out of it, in fact, but forever fine, forever sincere. He thought about this for a moment, and then he smiled at her. "Something like that," he agreed.

SISTERS

The Church Hall gym was full of boys. A stinging rain, almost sleet, almost snow, had driven the neighbourhood boys indoors, and all during the lesson the thud of basketballs reverberated through the building.

"You'd think it was some kind of an invasion..." As Martha spoke, yet another fusillade shook the walls of the little tutoring room. "Before was so quiet." She meant all those warm nights of September and October. Back then, hardly anyone had come into the Roxbury Bible Church. The noise had been mostly in the street, the Church Hall quiet as any school room.

"They's boys," said Darrylene shaking her head. Her dimpled hand swept out and grabbed the pencil that was rolling across the table. Beside her, Josie merely giggled.

Both sisters were short and plump. A pair of teddy bears, Martha had thought meeting them for the first time. At thirteen, Darrylene was the older by a year. She was also involved with a boy. Sleeping with him, according to the Tutoring Coordinator. Though "sleeping with" seemed to be a euphemism. The couple had been caught behind bleachers in the school gym, in various alleys, on the back seats of borrowed cars. Martha had found it hard to envision. Darrylene, round and childish, grappling with some boy in an alley, climbing up his thighs, absorbing his penis into her pudgy body?

You were supposed to be blasé about such things in the Movement. Martha knew that. But all through the fall she'd gone on wondering. Was the boyfriend one of those fast-talking teenagers she passed in the street, perpetually in orbit around someone's transistor? Or one of those lithe boys she saw leaping about the Church Hall gym?

She paused in the doorway sometimes to watch them. Young leopards, they seemed, with their sure feet and their shiny, muscular grins.

Now, during a lull in the noise, she began to correct her pupils' exercise in compound multiplication. Seated kneecap to kneecap at the wooden table, the three of them bent their heads together, casting puddles of shadow on the sheets of white paper. The room contained nothing other than the table and chairs and, shoved into one corner, several cartons filled with yellow plastic dishes.

"So, don't forget to change the sign," Martha warned. Darrylene leaned back in her chair. Her toffee-coloured eyes drifted from Martha to the ceiling. She had already got the problem right. But Josie screwed up her forehead and started to erase the numbers she had just written. "Because," said Martha, "once you reverse the numerator and the denominator, you..."

The door crashed open. A boy stood in the doorway. He didn't speak, and the girls didn't, and Martha, staring at him, forgot everything she'd imagined. For one thing, the boy in the doorway looked sick. His face was greasy and sweaty...her mother would have taken his temperature instantly...and his skin, for a black person, remarkably pale. The colour of mushrooms almost. He was skinny too. Below the cuffs of his sweater, the knobby bones of his wrists shone like coins.

On the other side of the table, Darrylene's chair scraped the floor angrily. "I axed you, boy..." Her voice as she stood up was a piercing falsetto. "I told you...you not going come here."

The boy's eyes swung toward her, but even as Martha jumped to her feet, Darrylene underwent a transformation. Her childish body arched into a covergirl pose. One stubby, vermilion-tipped hand floated to her hip; a come-hither smile bloomed on her face.

At her elbow, Josie doubled over, giggles spilling from her. "Shh," Martha said. "Shh."

But the boy's eyes were aimed at Darrylene. Lifting a thin hand, he snapped his fingers. Once, twice...the sound cracked between them like a whip. Martha looked from on to the other. Lovers. The smile had flown from Darrylene's face, She was staring open-mouthed at the boy, and he was staring back, grim as a little pirate king. It was like a movie. What would he do? Perhaps they... But already he had whirled, and now he was slipping back into the hall.

Gone. The room seemed suddenly empty, the smack of basketballs unbearably loud. Martha took a deep breath. She should do something, act like a teacher, say something.

But it was Josie who spoke, her voice still bunched with laughter. "That's be her boyfriend, Miss Martha."

Darrylene sighed. A sheen of sweat had appeared on her cheeks, and her eyes, as they drifted from Josie to Martha and then to the doorway, looked huge and unfocussed. Without speaking she turned and ran out of the room.

"Wait," called Martha. "Please. Wait..." From the hallway footsteps sounded in brief staccato, then were buried under an avalanche of basketballs.

In the Massachusetts of 1964, unmarried sex was not a legitimate pursuit. This was the ridiculous truth. Not even for grown-ups. Contraceptives were not for sale, so far as Martha knew, the pill obtainable only by the married or engaged, and even then you and the doctor had to pretend you were taking it to promote fertility.

Martha's roommate had had an abortion. Her boyfriend was a graduate student, uncertain about marriage and many other issues. The abortion had cost a terrific amount of money. Though the roommate's family was well-off, she had not dared ask them for help. The money had been borrowed by the boyfriend. The operation had taken place at a clinic in Pennsylvania. After it she had bled for a long time.

Martha herself had avoided sexual intercourse thus far. The consequences had seemed great, men unreliable. At least until Pierre. And about Pierre she was still holding her breath. He was dark-eyed and lean, her favourite combination, and he spoke with a French-Canadian accent that was satisfyingly foreign. "Do you know where is the liquor commission?" had been his first sentence. They were both standing in Harvard Square, she just emerged from the shop where she worked. The shop sold imported cookware, wisks and woks and long-handled wooden spoons. "Your hair is beautiful," he'd added. "The colour is like syrup." The wind was blowing, and her French twist, properly sleek and adult-looking while she'd set out the displays of enamelled casseroles, had just tumbled down the back of her neck.

Pierre smoked a great deal. That was another thing about him; he'd looked sophisticated standing there gesturing with his cigarette, the ribbon of smoke tracing little curls in the air. His "r's" emerged from somewhere deep in his throat. The sound "th" escaped him entirely; her name mutated into "Marta." They had a beer that night in Brattle Street and then went out the next night as well. He was at the Harvard Business School; his family had ambitions for him...both financial and political. He was the first son to be university educated, the first to study outside Quebec. The jewel of the family. He had explained all this with cheerful immodesty while attempting to unbutton her blouse. On the weekend they had driven out to Crane's Beach where the fall wind blew the rough grass flat and sand slithered into the pockets of their jeans. He was talking, confiding in her about his plans for when he returned to Montreal, and she had suddenly felt what she'd known only fleetingly before, the desire to melt herself into a man, to be his skin, to become his thoughts. Like a craving for candy, the feeling had stayed with her, teasing and persistent, and she came to discern in it a portent of sadness too, as though her future was now foreshortened, the end of the story in sight.

Darrylene no longer came regularly to tutoring sessions. When she did show up, she remained easy to teach, absorbing concepts as soon as Martha could put them forth, scribbling answers, then shoving her notebook across the table at Martha. "I gots it, I gots it!" Her smile lit the room.

On the other side of the table, oblivious to her sister's quicksilver performances (as they had all grown oblivious to the boom of basketballs), Josie crouched over her notebook, her jaw thrust forward in bulldog determination. Almost physically, she fought her way through compound fractions, then moved on to struggle with decimals. Each week she appeared bearing embattled pieces of paper, much-erased, much-folded, every square inch studded with figures. She also brought her graded school tests to Martha, who worked through the mistakes with her. The D's on these tests had begun to change, first to C's, and now, some of them, to B's.

About Darrylene's results, Martha was not so sure. Darrylene herself volunteered nothing during her infrequent visits, and Josie shook her head when asked. "She don't tell me." Gazing at Martha, her usually voluble eyes, smaller and more energetic than her sister's, were silent.

Just before report cards were due out, Martha got up her courage to see a gynaecologist. Getting off early from work, she took a subway and then a bus out to his clinic. The examination itself was brief, the doctor's hands cold, but he did not hurt her, and it was only subsequently, sitting in his office, that she began to feel panic, as though she were a little girl summoned for some incomprehensible crime to the inner and potentially inescapable confines of the principal's office.

Afterward she could recall the visit only in fragments. The name she'd appropriated for the occasion, the borrowed ring glittering on her finger, the doctor's seamed face as he listened to her story. Behind him the sun had reflected in brilliant rectangles off various framed diplomas. "And how soon do you plan to marry?" he'd said, touching the tips of his fingers together, left hand to right hand, in the shape of an arch. She had emerged warm with embarrassment (he could not have believed her for one minute), the precious prescription for the pill folded in her wallet.

This humiliation, this subterfuge, was sex. And sex would be other things too. She knew this from her roommate. A man's apartment. Alibis and soiled sheets. The triumph, slightly seedy, slightly ignoble, of breaking the rules and getting away with it. Sex would also be pleasure, she was sure, hot, skin to skin, animal pleasure. The kind she'd read about. The kind she wanted.

The week report cards were to be issued, the girls' mother asked Martha to dinner. News of the invitation was brought to the Church Hall by an excited Josie, her red-ribboned pigtails quivering with triumph. Martha had accepted immediately.

The family's apartment house stood on a side street a few blocks from the Church Hall. Like most of the tenements in the area, it rose five or six stories to a flat roof and, in the shine of the Roxbury street light, revealed myriad gouges and cracks. It looked, Martha decided as she picked her way along the snow-covered sidewalk, not unlike the old tin bread box her mother used to keep on the kitchen counter.

Inside the building, however, was nothing so cozy as bread. The air was acrid with the smell of rotting garbage. A single light bulb lit the stairwell, and in the cave-like dimness, Martha felt colder than she had outside. She thought of her own apartment back on Commonwealth Avenue, the comfiness of their living room couch, the taste of supper (toast with peanut butter melting around the edges was her favourite), and then, of course, there was later to think about too, meeting Pierre for coffee.

Only after she'd climbed four creaking flights did anticipation catch up with her. The mother's invitation had been an honour. Martha knew that. The family's living room further restored her confidence. Sofa, easy chair, mother and children…in the corner a big black and white television boomed like a drunken but cheerful guest. Here were the trappings of home. It hardly mattered that the room was tiny and windowless, the sofa sagging. On the floor, two little boys were playing with a saucepan and a tube of cardboard.

The mother had to step around them to greet Martha. She was short and round like her daughters and had milk chocolate skin. The hand she proffered was the same dimpled muffin of a hand too. But where their faces were open and unquestioning, hers was full of distractions, as if Martha, though welcome, had captured only a part of her attention.

"You just sit down here," she told Martha after they had shaken hands. Then she turned and left the room. The little boys scrambled after her.

The mother's nod had indicated the sofa, and Martha seated herself on it now. The springs nudged her buttocks in retaliation. Smoothing her skirt (to look mature, she had worn her best navy gabardine suit), she glanced around the room. Beside the television was a pile of calendars and behind them, propped against the wall, what looked like several artist's canvasses, their ragged edges nailed around wooden frames.

"See, Miss Martha, see…" Josie shot into the room followed by Darrylene waving two cardboard folders. "I gots mostly all B's! And Darrylene here, she pass in every subject!" The sofa wheezed and rocked as they bounced down on either side of Martha.

She inspected the report cards. "But this is wonderful," she told them, raising her voice against the television. "Both of you. Wonderful." Was it possible those hours in the Church Hall sitting room had made this happen? That she Martha had made a difference? For a second the tips of her fingers tingled. On either side of her the spicy scent of their hair lotion was in the air. Breathing it in she felt warmed.

"What I tell them..." The mother was standing in the doorway, her body opulent beneath the folds of her black dress. Behind her, portions of sink and stove were visible. "You got to..." The rest of her words were drowned by a burst of laughter from the television.

"Excuse me?" said Martha.

"Educated." The mother enunciated each syllable. "That's what I tell them. You got to get educated. Otherwise..." Once more her voice was overridden by the television.

"Mama...Mama...?" One of the little boys was peering around the shelter of the mother's body. He reached up and tugged on her dress. "Mama? When's supper, Mama?"

"Soon enough," she told him.

And indeed the smell of frying had begun to fill the living room. Hamburger, Martha guessed, and onions. Her mouth watered. She'd had only an apple for lunch. To distract herself, she glanced around once more at the paintings. They leaned against the wall like so many discarded objects.

Shaking off the little boys, the mother stepped into the room. She lowered herself into the armchair, then reached over and turned down the volume of the television. Gesturing at the paintings, she fixed Martha with her deepset, brown eyes. "My husband. He's be painting those." Her voice was solemn, as though the issue was a particularly serious one. Her husband, she said, was working the nightshift this month. He painted when he could, mostly portraits, although he had tried outdoors places too. She did not offer to show the paintings, and the only one Martha could see full-on was of a woman, nude from the waist up. The woman's hair curved like a strip of black cloth around the sides of her face. Her skin was a smooth, milk-chocolate brown.

"It's you, isn't it?" said Martha, suddenly certain. On either side of her, giggles erupted.

Now that she looked, the features were unquestionably the mother's. Yet the face in the painting seemed lifeless, like an icon or a mask; the broad, down-curving lips and heavy-lidded eyes conveying no emotion, offering no recognition. No, what made Martha's cheeks grow warm as she stared, what gave away the woman in the painting...because, surely, something did...were the breasts. Like fruit on a tray...bounteous was the word that popped into her head...as if by their very position they couldn't help but offer themselves.

"Worst is my feet gets asleep..." the mother said.

"Your feet?"

"Sitting on that bitty stool whiles he's painting."

"Mama, we hungry."

The mother's glance swung around to rest on the little boys who had sidled in and were leaning on her chair arm. Then she shook her head, not exactly at them, and went on talking. "He have other models, but I'm his favourite one." She sounded proud. "You just got to leave go what you're doing," the mother added. "You got to pay attention to a man's dream." Martha pressed her hands to her cheeks...how hot they were.

Afterwards, Martha was not sure why that was the night she first went to bed with Pierre. Her cheeks were still hot when she met him for coffee. "They were really nice to me," she told him. "She talked about her husband. She sounded so wise." He listened, his eyes bright and amused, while she recited the events of the evening. Then he drove them back to her apartment.

The roommate was out on a date. That, of course, made it possible. That was the coincidence. But the desire was something else. Sex? Love? A wish to be overtaken and pinned down, defined in some way? She didn't know.

They had made no preparations, she and Pierre. He had no condom; she had no diaphragm. She wasn't even sure if she could have bought one in another state. Didn't they have to be fitted, or prescribed, or something? Nor had she yet had the courage to fill her prescription for the pill.

"You are almost to your period, no?" He whispered this, pushing her down onto the bed.

"Yes," she whispered back. "A day or two, I think." His hands were unhooking her nylons from her garter belt. The outline of his head blocked the light from the hall, and suddenly in the blending darkness she imagined Darrylene, her clothes thrown open, her back pressed into the gritty, varethaned floor of the school gym as Martha's was pressed into the mattress. Did Darrylene too lie waiting like this, while her lover brought his weight and warmth, his hardness down upon her?

"You smell funny..." Pierre was sniffing her neck and hair.

"What...? Oh, the dinner..." She sighed and slid her arms up around his shoulders. How soft his skin was over the bone and muscle, like silk over stone. The dinner had turned out to be a slippery goulash that skated about on the plate, spilling shiny bits of itself into her gabardine lap. The taste had been more peppery than she'd expected.

"Like a hamburger." Pierre's breath was warm in her ear.

Afterward, he sat in the living room, smoking a cigarette and leafing through one of her James Baldwin novels. He liked the fact that she was always reading. He'd told her this. And he liked what he called her civil rights affair too; he was interested in knowing what went on. He bought local newspapers and sent away for *The New York Times* (it was good for his English). But he thought her silly about politics. "Inévoluée," he called her.

"The tutoring is nice," he said. "But what does it change for them? They are still black."

"It's giving them choices," she'd protested. If you knew more, you had more choices. Wasn't that what everyone said in the Movement? Freedom came from choice. She Martha had it all. White, college educated... He had interrupted her monologue by laughing, then kissing her.

Now he glanced up at her as she stood in the bathroom doorway wrapped in her towel. "You are beautiful like that...with your hair wet." He gestured with his cigarette. "This book, by the way, this man, he is very interesting."

She smiled. She felt beautiful...that was what sex could do for you even if it did seem to hurt. She still felt a little uncomfortable, though Pierre assured her this would pass. "Which man?" she said.

"The writer of this." He tapped his knee with the book. "Do you know people like this in your tutoring?"

"Like James Baldwin? I don't think so..." She considered the girls' mother. There were no characters like her in Baldwin's books, were there? "Of course, I didn't meet the father." Maybe he would have been more like James Baldwin. An artist, after all. Though being black he was not so likely to have the chance to be a real artist, to show his work in a gallery. Who would come to find him there in Roxbury? Maybe he didn't know about galleries.

"In Montreal the winters are not like this."

This was two months later. Martha, safely on the pill, had gained ten pounds. She'd had to buy new skirts and bras. Her thighs strained against the fabric that covered them; her breasts felt swollen and weighty and, in bed with Pierre, rather grand. As though, infused with the daily dose of estrogen and indeed with Pierre himself, everything about her had become more intensely female. Pierre did not mind the added pounds. She was like an apple, he said, round and shiny. Old lovers now, he and she were heading out for coffee after an hour in her apartment, picking their way, hand in gloved hand, along the strip of snowy park that bisected Commonwealth Avenue.

Pierre let go her hand to turn up his jacket collar. "In Montreal," he told her, "they lift the snow out of the big streets and take it away." He made a lifting gesture with both arms.

She could see Montreal…like Tolstoy's St. Petersburg. Mounds of clean, never-melting snow edging chalky streets. Women in fur-trimmed coats, men with dark hair and eyes like Pierre's, and everyone speaking English with funny accents. (She did not think of them as speaking French, though of course down the road French would be something to learn. Pierre had said he would teach her, but perhaps she would need a tutor as well.)

Where they were walking now, the slush-covered pavement was populated with dogs leashed firmly to their owners, and women minding baby carriages, and couples like herself and Pierre. Through the traffic that ran along either side of the park, she could see the rows of tall stone houses. Apartments had been carved from the insides of these houses, their plumbing and fixtures allowed to deteriorate, as Martha well knew, but the façades—from this distance anyway—were wonderfully elaborate and old-fashioned. All those cornices and arches and balustrades. It was fun to live on such a street.

Glancing back over her shoulder, she could just spot the window of her own apartment. High up, in what must have been servants' quarters, the window was wide enough for her and her roommate to lean out and laugh themselves to ecstasy over whatever was going on in the street below. Once, in a strong wind, they had sailed tiny, makeshift kites out that window, another time…but here Pierre's hand closed around hers. His grip was firm…the park benches and the baby carriages snapped back into view…and turning to meet his smile…how dark his eyes were, with little stars in them like the sky at night…she ignored the sudden heaviness in her stomach.

Pierre formed the same opinion of the Boston summer as he had of the Boston winter. Inferior. Too humid. Too messy. "The spring was nice," he allowed sadly. "But this..." With a wave of his hand, he indicated the squadron of flies that circled the light fixture on her living room ceiling.

He had arrived bearing a semi-chilled bottle of California Chablis. They were sharing this, drinking it from coffee mugs, while they packed up her possessions...books (Baldwin and Kerouac, Ferlinghetti, a much-underlined paperback copy of *Anna Karenina* from a college course), clothes, records (Odetta, Joan Baez, Aaron Copland's *Appalachian Spring*, to which they had once made love), a set of wooden spoons and an apron from her shop (a gift from the proprietor). She fitted the assortment of records into the carton and then glanced over at him. "You could become a citizen here, you know. When you're married to me. You could stay in America...."

He laughed. Then he got up and came over to where she knelt. "Montreal *is* in America. We have something like your Movement even." But not my Movement, she thought of saying. Not my anything. But the words seemed unfair, untrue even...she and he were engaged, after all; his life would be her life...and then he was bending over her, the warmth of him closing around her, his voice rumbling gently in her ear. "In summer," he told her, "Montreal is the nicest city in the world."

In the summer, Boston was a nice city too, wasn't it? Martha thought so, though she hadn't argued. It was hard to argue with Pierre (he listened, but then when she'd finished, he just smiled and ruffled her hair or kissed the back of her neck). There were tourists these days in the shop, shy tourists and cheerful ones, more polite quite often than the local customers. And then there were the long, rose-tinted evenings, the walks around Boston Garden and Harvard Square, softball games and sometimes free concerts in the grassy park that ran along the Boston side of the Charles River.

Tutoring had ended with the school year, and when Martha borrowed Pierre's car one evening to drive over to Roxbury and say goodbye to the family, she had not seen Josie for nearly six weeks and Darrylene for a good deal longer.

As it turned out, neither Darrylene nor the father was at the apartment when Martha arrived. The two little boys were there though, and there was the same smell of cooking. Since the winter the mother seemed to have grown larger. Her body moved, as Martha imagined a transatlantic ship might move, with ponderous sway, from stove to drawer to cupboard, her hips and her ample buttocks rounding out the skirt of her housedress. Her arms, as she handed down cups and spoons to Josie, then hefted a sack of sugar, were big as footballs.

To keep out of the way, Martha did what she did in her own mother's kitchen. She leaned against the doorframe and talked about herself. "It's hard leaving Boston," she confided after she'd explained her plans. "All my friends. Everything...in Quebec I won't even be able to vote." Her first ballot had been cast the previous fall for President Johnson, running against Senator Goldwater from Arizona, a man whose ideas seemed as parental and quaint as the antique ring on her finger. The ring, fashioned of amethysts and white gold, had belonged to Pierre's grandmother. The grandmother lived in Quebec City; she had borne eleven children. Twisting the ring slowly around her finger, Martha watched the stones blur into a single smear of purple.

The mother had been spooning mounds of sugar and instant coffee into the cups. Now she poured boiling water into each one and set the pan back on the stove before glancing up. Her shrug was elaborate, the suddenly visible palms of her hands startling in their paleness.

"Miss Martha? Miss Martha?" Josie was tapping Martha on the hand. "I gots a thing to show you, Miss Martha."

"A man," said the mother, "going always be like that." She sounded impatient, as if Martha had failed to appreciate some obvious and unchangeable truth.

"Miss Martha...I just remember it." Josie's face was excited.

"Sure, Josie," said Martha. The sensation of tears was nearly gone. Josie had already rushed from the room. A moment later she returned and handed her report card to Martha.

The A stood out like a flag. "Josie! An A in math!" Martha read down the list of subjects. Every other grade was B or B+.

The mother came over to put her arm around her daughter. Side by side, they stood smiling up at Martha. "I and her father thanks you," the mother said in her formal voice.

"Oh, no," said Martha. "No, don't thank me. I didn't do the studying, I didn't take the tests..." Embarrassed, she stared at their faces and searched for something else to say. "What about Darrylene? How did she do?"

The smile fell from the mother's face. And she turned her head aside, as if to hide the place where the smile had rested. "Oh, she fine, she fine..." Her voice had gone flat.

Had Darrylene flunked? Had she run away with that boy? With uncertain hands, Martha received her cup of coffee and followed the mother into the living room. Propped against the wall was another painting, also of a nude, though this one appeared unfinished. The woman's face had no features. Chin propped on her hand, shoulders rounded, she lay on her side. A sort of low table had been sketched in as her resting place.

A quarter of an hour later, no wiser on the subject of Darrylene, Martha made her way down the dark stairway. The coffee, though heavily sugared, had been so strong she could still taste it. She emerged from the building onto a sidewalk crowded with people. The whole neighbourhood, it seemed, had come out to enjoy the brilliant summer evening. Sunlight slanted down between the buildings, illuminating people as if they were stage figures just come to life. Suddenly...as though she too lived here, had spent all day in the tiny apartment...nothing was more wonderful than to be out-of-doors.

Squinting against the sunlight, she worked her way through the crowd on the sidewalk. Then, as she was unlocking Pierre's car, she spotted Darrylene. The girl stood in a bunch of eight or ten teenagers half-way along the block. For a moment Martha stared up the street. She waved once, but no one in the group responded.

A few minutes later, she drove the car up flush with them and, leaning across the seat, rolled down the righthand window. The teenagers were laughing and shouting at one another. Even now they paid no attention to Martha. Darrylene lounged against a light standard smoking ostentatiously. She wore rolled up blue pants and a big, loose man's shirt. The others, boys and girls, wore pants too and shirts or T shirts, some with the sleeves torn out. The skinny boyfriend was not among them.

"Hello!" shouted Martha. Faces turned toward her, and each went immediately blank. Martha waited. The moment gathered silence until, finally, recognition lit the face of the older sister. She stepped forward out of the group, and it was then that Martha saw the convex curve of her belly pushing out the folds of the oversize shirt.

Smiling, Darrylene bent down and thrust her face through the window. "Hi, Miss Martha." No embarrassment tinged her expression, nothing but a child's friendly lack of curiosity.

Heat was flooding up the back of Martha's neck. "I came, I mean, I wanted to say goodbye. I'm moving away. To Quebec."

"Kwuh...bec..." Darrylene drawled as if humouring a child. The syllables conveyed no meaning. Her face, still smiling, receded from the window. She stood up, and in a single, graceful sweep (reminiscent of her mother, though the gesture was definitely movie star) she lifted her arm and flicked the ashes from her cigarette.

"I can't leave." The words came without thinking. "I live here...this. How can I just leave?"

Pierre was washing his car in the driveway of his tutorial professor's house in Cambridge. The driveway was paved with flat red bricks; dandelions and little tufts of grass grew up in the spaces between them. Martha had been lying on the grass, watching him and feeling wonderfully warm and inert, as though each cell of her body was imbued with the residue of pleasure. Now, stricken by her own words, she sat up and stared at Pierre. He had taken off his shirt, and the centre of his back between his shoulder blades gleamed with sweat.

He turned and smiled over at her. "Because you have to be with me," he said.

"Oh," she said still staring at him. How tanned he had become. Almost, his skin had turned a true brown. She had told him the story of Darrylene. "She'll never get free," she added now. "She'll have a million babies and, if she gets work at all, a nothing job..."

"Your student, the girl who is pregnant?"

"She was so smart, Pierre."

Pierre wrung out the sponge and then applied more liquid carwash to the car, which was blue and white and, along its sides, scarred with rust. (It looked like a Chevrolet but was called a Laurentian.) Then he glanced around at Martha again. "But she is still smart," he said gravely. "She can have another tutor, yes?"

She stared at his puzzled, cheerful face. "You don't understand," she told him. "She doesn't even know what she's getting into. She hasn't a clue. You should have seen her..."

The round brown arm lifting and flicking, the little spray of ash drifting down...for a second Martha held her breath; she could see it all clearly...the crowd of teenagers framed in the car window and the evening light shining on them. Then Pierre began to wash down the bulbous hood of the car. As he rubbed, his knuckles whitened, and drops of water spattered across the driveway. His arm swept back and forth over the dark gleaming surface of the hood.

Beneath the palms of her hands and her bare calves, the grass was cool and damp. This sadness would go away, no doubt, this strange feeling that something inside her was changed or even gone. Sighing she lay back. Clouds had begun to edge across the sky, dimming the afternoon. In her mind the sunlit Roxbury street was fading too, its edges already tinged sepia and parchment gold like a photograph taken long ago and pasted down in an album, a memento...and this was the strangest feeling of all...a memento, no longer of her own, but of someone else's past.

The Jaguar Temple

They had warned Beth about the water, the salads. Not even a wet toothbrush, they had said firmly. Did it matter then that she chewed up the ice in her drink—an awful local whisky—while the Mayor of the city and the President of something else gave those boring speeches and the dignitaries hustled about the gilded reception room hugging and even kissing each other? Defiantly crunching a mouthful of ice, she rolled her eyes at Bob, who responded by laying a hand on her shoulder. The hand was heavy, like something ominous. A warning. She was not to make a scene. But the answer to her question, if she had asked it, was yes. It did matter.

"They" had known what they were talking about—at least insofar as the water was concerned—and vengeance came swiftly in the night. While Bob slept, she traipsed back and forth to the bathroom, throwing it all up, the dinner not much liked, the wine, the local whisky drunk to blur the evening. Kneeling on the damp tiles, for perhaps the fifth or sixth time, she felt a child's desperation that the night might never end. But of course it did, and she ended up in the airport waiting room the next morning with everyone else while the Mayor gave yet another speech.

It wouldn't do to disappoint these people. Bob had said this by way of persuasion. He himself was hammering out the best deal he could, working on the Mayor as hard as possible. And she, Beth, should try to pull herself together. These people took it hard if you got poisoned by their food or water. It shamed them. And besides this whole excursion had been set up for the company delegation. She would just have to show.

"Come on, hon," he said finally, throwing a massive arm around her shoulder. It was the closest he came to pleading.

In the insipid light of dawn, his face looked featureless, almost monolithic, as he gazed down at her. The arm was weighing her down—like a yoke, she thought then—but she had nodded, stipulating only that she would eat nothing.

"Right-o," agreed Bob. "Nothing goes in; nothing comes out." He laughed and gave her shoulder a final squeeze.

Now in the carpeted, windowless VIP lounge, which smelled of cleaning fluid and coffee, they all stood patiently—the tall, pale Canadians beside their stouter and darker hosts—while the Mayor went on and on, promising that the day would be fascinating, the trip unforgettable.

He swayed when he spoke, and his round face bunched into grimaces and smiles. "These ancient cities," he assured them, "they are the wonder of the western world." As he spoke, one of his secretaries circulated through the group handing out cups of coffee.

"Mayor's mistress," murmured the voice of the Chairman, more or less in Beth's ear. She could feel his warm breath. "Mayor's fancy lady," he reiterated. And indeed the woman's aggressive makeup—garish now in the morning light—and her tight green dress and spike heels did seem to define her as a non-wife. But still, it was hard to know who was what in the world, and especially here. She glanced across at the Mayor's wife, who was sitting on a sofa with two of the other local ladies. Although the room was cool enough, all three were fanning themselves vigorously as they waited for the Mayor's speech to end itself. The fans were real; Beth could imagine the little stir of air each produced. Forbearance was so obviously the virtue of these women, that she felt a sudden sting of admiration for the flamboyance of the Mayor's secretary.

"You will see the famous Jaguar Temple," announced the Mayor. "The Maya were very religious people...always making their buildings another time..." He beamed and nodded at his audience.

Beth's guidebook, which she had been glancing into surreptitiously, was somewhat clearer on this subject.

The temples of Tikal were built and destroyed and rebuilt on the same foundations an untold number of times. It appears that the Mayan culture rose and collapsed by the lives of its leaders, who were perhaps its chief priests. There may also have been dynasties...

The guns went off while the Mayor was still emoting. Afterwards Beth had no idea why she had been gazing away toward the doorway at that particular point. It was an ordinary moment. Their guards stood, as they had on every occasion, just outside the room. People were moving across the space of the doorway; most were hurrying. As she looked, the guards' arms swung down, and the butts of their guns rose. Like a railway crossing gate, was Beth's last thought before the sharp, spattering sound erupted and the guards' backs suddenly filled the doorway. Inside the room no one moved. No one spoke. The Mayor's mouth remained frozen around one of his promises. There was another spattering sound, far quieter than she would have imagined gunfire might be, and a single long scream. Then the doors slammed shut, as if the scream itself were an offense, and around her voices rose in an excited swarm.

In the next moment the doors reopened briefly to admit a small man in a white safari suit. The small man looked wildly around once and then worked his way through the group fending off questions until he reached the Mayor, who immediately grabbed his shoulders as if to shake information out of him.

Both men spoke at once, gesturing violently beneath the watchful eyes of Bob. Standing more than a head taller than either, he loomed over their discussion like a big brother. Finally, the Mayor took a backward step and held up his hands for quiet. Reinforcing this plea, Bob and the small man glared around at the group from their respective heights.

When the babble had died down, the Mayor clasped his raised hands together like a supplicant. "There is no problem," he cried wringing his hands for all to see and then suddenly flashing the palms of them at the crowd. "No problem! We will leave very soon. An unfortunate incident." He glanced at the small man, and some decision seemed to pass between them. "We will go now please. It will be a pleasant day. You will see much. Our country has a fascinating history..." People began shuffling toward the outside exit. Beth moved to follow Bob's wide back. And as the last of their group passed out into the brilliant morning, the resonant voice of the Mayor's secretary could be heard wishing everyone a pleasant journey.

"But someone was shot," Beth said to Bob as they shuffled down the aisle of the DC3. "They screamed."

"Not a hell of a lot we can do about it." Bob's head was slightly inclined to one side—he was too tall to stand up straight—and his eyes were casting about over her head to see how the seating arrangements would unfold. And she had to admit he was right enough—this while being handed into a window seat—that there was most definitely not a hell of a lot he or she could do. Now he indicated with a jerk of his head that he would be moving on, and she nodded her acceptance. Things always, it seemed, ended up this way. Bob always had to take care of some bit of business, tie up some loose end.

She had just pulled the guidebook out of her bag when the Chairman dropped heavily into the seat beside her.

"Pretty girl all alone." He fumbled with the seat belt and then snapped it closed. "What a day, eh? Happens all the time in these countries." His hand settled on hers. "No discipline." He chuckled complacently. "British have the right idea. Don't arm their police..." He released her hand as the plane lurched and then began to move steadily. "Confidentially, we're going to have a tough time here...can't say it's my cup of tea, but your young man's all set to do the job..."

"I guess so," said Beth. The Chairman often mentioned Bob's youth, while Bob in more or less the same tone was forever referring to the Chairman as "a great old guy." They were always needling one another. Yet they liked each other. Everybody said so. The Chairman had, after all, more or less chosen Bob for his successor. Everybody, with varying degrees of envy or pessimism, said that too. Perhaps that was why the Chairman chose so often—three or four times in the last few days—to sit beside Beth. It was not a privilege she would have sought. She was tired of being patted, and besides that the Chairman was very fond of his own voice. It wasn't, in fact, until the roar of taking off silenced him that she managed to begin reading.

> *In this narrow land between two oceans, the Maya carved out a civilization remarkable for its ritual and organization as well as for the grandeur of its cities. Infra-red photographs taken from satellites show a network of irrigation canals now buried beneath a jungle that stretches north and south and shore to shore across...*

The DC3 was levelling off. Already they had climbed above the mud-coloured hills that surrounded the city and were swinging slowly around to the north. From her window Beth strained to see the ocean, either ocean. She wanted a border. She wanted some definition to this country where guns went off at the airport and fever and sickness were the result of an ordinary drink. But, though now and again she stared very hard, no edge to the land appeared. Gradually, the folded hills below them became more convoluted, the valleys deeper and darker, until the colour of the land itself began to change. First to a pale, even green...then to a richer hue, a strong, tropical green.

The jungle has covered Tikal and her sister cities for more than ten centuries. All the sites were abandoned around 900 A.D. No evidence exists...

The Chairman's hand was patting her arm this time. She could smell his pepperminty, old-man's breath. "Now, my dear, I don't want you to worry..."

"Not worry?" echoed Beth. "Not worry? I suppose you and Bob will just shoot a few of them back?"

The Chairman's wiry eyebrows arched in surprise. "Now, my dear," he said in the indulgent but reproving tone one used with a child who had been allowed along on the adults' expedition. "Now, my dear, you're not as a rule a sarcastic woman... It isn't good to pay too much attention to these matters in a country like this. Why I remember back when Laura was alive..."

As he talked, she freed her arm by the expedient of reaching up and pressing her palm against the window. The misty imprint faded in a few seconds. But the glass was divinely cool against her hot skin. No doubt then, she had a fever, along with this diffuse and seemingly permanent headache.

Far below them now she could see, if she looked hard, the narrow brown line of a highway winding up and down the jungle green mountains. The Chairman's voice rasped on like an overtone to the drone of the engine. And all at once she missed her husband, so much and so sharply it was as if he had died young and she were alone. Bob, she would have liked to say to him, pressing companionably against his solid arm. Bob, look. It's like the legend of a highway. She would have liked to say this to him, or to someone, though not to the Chairman. A pathway for pilgrims and for warriors. Thoughtfully, she turned a page in the guidebook.

The temples of Tikal were built for worship and for sacrifice. Victims were tied, arms bound to their legs as can be seen in etchings on the sides of the temples, and slaughtered on the highest platforms of the temples. The priests sacrificed prisoners taken in war, it is believed, slicing their throats...

I want to die. Like a bubble, the thought rose to the surface of her mind and popped away. She paused for a second, blinking, and then went on reading.

The plane landed on a single runway, thundering past a few sheds, one with "beba Coca Cola" painted on its side, then bumping gradually to a stop at the far end of the runway.

In the minibus Beth went on reading.

Only a sixteenth of Tikal has yet been excavated. Indeed, as is true of all the ancient Mayan cities, most of its treasures lie untouched beneath the jungle.

The words jumped in front of her eyes, and she looked up just as the minibus plunged into the jungle. High over the road now, the trees closed together in a giant archway. "So dark," murmured one of the ladies. There were answering murmurs. The minibus jerked and swayed. Inside the heat was growing intense.

"Is the jungle," announced the guide. No one else spoke.

After another five minutes, the minibus bumped off the road into a cleared space and stopped. Still no sunlight reached down to touch them as they squeezed out of the bus. "Been more comfortable in a Sherman tank," grumbled the Chairman. He was, she noticed, massaging his shoulders and only gradually did he seem to straighten up to his full height. He looked, standing there in the clearing, like an old man.

Above them, in the high, dim space a bird flew out of the leaves, and then another one. On the far side of the clearing, a wall rose behind the trees. Was this their goal?

But it was not a wall, Beth realized as they crossed the clearing. The guide was herding them toward the back of a building. They filed along a path beside its rough, porous-looking stone, then around a corner, and suddenly the jungle fell away. Before them stretched a huge grass-covered space, larger than a football field. At either end loomed stone temples, taller than the surrounding jungle. Buildings of the same grey stone lined one side of the grassy field. The other side finished in a series of stone terraces and beyond them Beth glimpsed more temples. This ancient plaza reduced the jungle to a pleasant, green background. A few other people, tourists like themselves, draped with cameras and canvas bags, wandered about or sat on the stone terraces gazing up at the temples.

Slowly now, their group set out across the sunlit grass. When was it, thought Beth, trying to place the time of the city as her feet trod the spongy grass. The early Middle Ages? She found the answer in her guidebook.

> *In the cities of the ancient Maya, all the buildings are of an age, that is to say, about one thousand years.*

Yet, perhaps because its history was unrecorded, its stories untold, it seemed older, this city. Infinitely older.

The sun struck sharply on the top of her head, and Beth felt dizzy for a moment as she walked. Still, there was no question but that she was feeling better. Perhaps the humidity had leached the illness out of her...the jungle air that had closed over them as they'd emerged from the plane, air so water-laden it seemed that they moved beneath the surface of a lake. Or maybe it was the guide who had cured her.

While the others were being served lunch in one of the sheds, he had brought her a mug of steaming tea. "From the allspice tree," he had explained. "Is wanderfool tea." And she had drunk it all, her eyes half-closed, her head adrift in the pungent steam. Perhaps it *was* the tea...working its magic now in the ancient city.

Ahead of her the group paused and gathered around the guide. "Here!" he cried. His arms extended upward in ecstasy. "Here is the famous Jaguar Temple!" Behind him the grey stones marched upward like a giant staircase, insanely steep. "Two hundred thirty feet high," announced the guide. Halfway up a lone tourist clung to the tiered stones. At the summit a narrow platform encircling a hut built of the same stone crowned the temple. Beth could see a doorway in the centre of the hut, dark as the entrance to a cave.

> *At the top of the stairway, the high priests waited for the procession that climbed the temple bearing the victims. Here the leaders sacrificed to the Mayan gods in the ancient ritual...*

Beth saw herself, arms bound, waiting on that platform, alone above the crowd and every eye gazing up to the place where she stood.

"Is not known what happen to the Maya." The guide shrugged and gestured to indicate the unsolvability of this mystery. Sweat dripped from his spiky hair. "All things are ending, no?" He shrugged again. Plague and famine and war, he seemed to imply. Or just plain boredom. How many times can you tear down and rebuild the same temple? In the end it comes down to tourists.

"And now if you wish, we climb the temple, the Jaguar Temple...like the old priests?" He looked around at his charges. The ladies, fans gently waving, shook their heads in unison. Too hot. Too steep. Some of the men were volunteering to stay behind with the ladies, and others were stepping forward, to be counted. Bob, surprisingly, shook his head.

"Don't like heights...vertigo, you call it. Don't mind skiing, but this kind of thing..." He laughed heartily, but Beth saw the flush on his neck. I should stay behind with him, she told herself. It's what he expects. But I want to climb it, insisted another voice inside her. She glanced over at their guide and nodded before the shocked wife's voice inside her could contradict.

"I'll never get the chance again," she apologized to Bob. "It's such a chance..."

Bob's eyes stayed on her for a second and then slid off. "Right-o," he said. "Fantastic place!"

The Chairman caught up with Beth at the foot of the Jaguar Temple. "Spunky gal," he told her. "Just how I feel myself. Last chance." She glanced at him in surprise, but he was looking up at their goal. The steps were steep and high, almost a foot each. A chain, anchored into the stone by iron spikes, bisected the stairway and served as a kind of railing. The steps themselves were worn and jagged, broken in places. From this point she could no longer see the doorway at the top. There was a moment of hesitation. Who would go first? Six of them had elected to climb. The guide, Beth and the Chairman, two other company men who were determined presumably to get the most out of the trip, and the Mayor himself, who may have felt the exigencies of good hospitality. It was he who began the ascent, scrambling cautiously upward step by step, alternately grasping the chain and clutching at the step above him. Beth went after the two company men. She was followed by the Chairman and their guide. The sinuous chain seemed precarious to her, and after the first few steps she moved sideways away from the chain to where the steps were less worn. Now, like an animal, she could clamber up on all fours. After this she climbed without stopping or looking down, in the steady rhythm of a trotting dog, until she could pull herself panting but triumphant over the lip onto the platform

The Mayor's hand helped her to her feet. Behind him the heads of the other two peered like cautious children from the doorway of the stone hut. The height of it was only five feet. Stooping she stepped into the blackness. Behind her came the sound of wheezing, the scrape of heel on stone, the Chairman's breathy voice. "Some climb." In the dark he sounded plaintive.

More scraping. "Is very dark, no?" The guide's voice. Then click, and a circle of yellow light was stamped on the lines of a jaguar crouched in the stone wall. It had been there all along. The light swung around, and a second jaguar prowled on the opposite wall. "Two of them!" declared the guide. "The jaguar was the Mayan symbol of power, strength and power." He switched off the light. There was a general shuffling toward the doorway, and suddenly a sharp odour of sweat filled the darkness. The smell of human fear, abject and painful, a last manifestation perhaps...and Beth thought again of the ancient victims.

Emerging, she took a deep breath and then edged carefully after the others along the stone wall of the hut. Looking down was unbearable, empty space waiting to be fallen into. But the outward view took away her fear. Over the treetops, a layer of puffy green pierced here and there by the summits of other temples, they could look across miles of jungle. Like the priests of old, without connection, they surveyed the world below, the little moving figures, the grass, the lesser temples.

This was how it would have been. This wonderful godlike view that was now Beth's. This view that could belong only to a priest.. Better, to be a priest. Much better. To have the power and the indifference. She drew in another deep breath, feeling her ribs expand.

Beyond the terraces they could see another plaza surrounded by more temples. A great city then. She felt its importance suddenly, imagined the crowds of people moving across the huge squares, pausing near the temples, stopping to chat on the terraces, the vivid composite life of a city. The guide pointed out a small open courtyard at the edge of the farther plaza. "You see these walls? They are for the boll game."

"Bull game?" The Chairman peered over Beth's shoulder at the guide.

"Ball. Ball game," said one of the other men. "Yes?"

The guide nodded. Now he had their attention. "Yes. The ancient Maya, they play the boll games like us also. But..." He held up his finger and paused dramatically. "Is different one way! The team which has lose the game, she is all keel!"

"All keel?"

"Killed," explained the Mayor. "All killed. It was part of the ritual."

"Wow, rough sport."

"Some game!" They all shook their heads and went back to exclaiming over the view.

"Worth the climb...but I sure wouldn't mind a helicopter now," said one of the company men.

Looking straight down again, Beth suffered a gulp of fear. Several people stood at the base of the stairway, apparently waiting their turn to climb.

"Is time for descend," their guide announced as he too noticed the people waiting. This time he went first, demonstrating the proper method. Both hands grasping the chain, he backed down step by step, his body extended nearly flat against the steps. The two company men went next, one after the other. Beth retreated from the edge, wishing that she were safe on the grass below, or even part way down. The bigger of the company men had just taken his first downward step. He wasn't, of course, so large and imposing as Bob, but a tall heavy man all the same. In his grip the iron stake seemed to waver slightly, but before she was sure, he had let go and moved a step below it. The Mayor went next, and then the Chairman moved forward and knelt.

"I will go beneath you, my dear," he said starting to lower himself over the edge of the platform. "Be careful."

Beth nodded, wondering if he meant to catch her should she fall. The thought made her want to laugh. The Chairman plucking her out of the air and gallantly bearing her down those impossible stairs. And she nearly missed seeing the uppermost stake slide out of the stones as the Chairman's hand grasped the chain a few inches below it.

"Look out!" Her voice sprang into the empty air.

A look of utter surprise came over the Chairman's features. His hand opened, releasing the treacherous chain. Fortunately for him most of his weight rested on his feet, and after a few seconds of desperate scrabbling, he got hold of the steps, his fingers digging frantically into available cracks. The stake with the length of chain clattered down over the stone. It struck the Mayor's back just as he grabbed his section of chain. His hands jerked sharply on the chain. The next stake, the one above the Mayor's hands, now wavered in its turn and then slid smoothly out of its groove to join the clattering descent of the first stake.

Abruptly cut loose, the Mayor reared backward into space still clutching the traitorous chain. For an instant he hung in the air. Below him the other three men scrambled sideways away from the path of the chain; the tourists on the ground were backing away from the base of the temple. Each of these things happened in the slow insane time sequence of a nightmare. Now the Mayor was falling, then bouncing off a step, then falling again. Above him the stakes pulled out one by one, and the whole confusion—body, stakes and chain—slid and rolled, down and down, until with one final horrible bounce the Mayor landed on the grassy earth. The clatter of metal on stone continued for another second, and then an instant of stillness filled the plaza. No sound, no movement, until a thin wail rose like the ghost of ancient sorrow from the tableau of disaster below. Suddenly a sort of exhilaration welled up in Beth. She had seen it, the incredible plunge. Almost, she longed for an instant replay. So terrible the fall, so thrilling... No, terrible, terrible. She shook her head. Terrible. But the sensation had swept her clean. It was difficult to focus. Pay attention, she told herself. There was the Chairman still clinging frozen to the stone steps. Dropping onto her hands and knees she stretched out flat on her stomach along the platform and extended her hand to him. His scratched, veiny hand closed around her fingers, and stiffly as though recently injected with old age, he regained the platform, hauling himself up over the edge. Then side by side they sat on the stony rim, as if on a raft in the sky. Below them the Mayor's body lay under the coils of the chain like a fallen doll on the grass. From everywhere across the plaza little figures appeared running. A few light cries reached them, but no words, and neither of them considered descending. They huddled together, the last survivors they both felt.

"Christ Jesus," said the Chairman. And then after a minute, he added, "I hate being old." His voice was so bleak that Beth wondered whether he was seeking comfort. But she made no move. They watched the tiny figures kneeling beside the Mayor. After a minute one of the minibuses appeared at the far corner of the plaza and came bouncing over the grass. "You couldn't have done anything," Beth remarked.

But he shook his head. "I goddamn well hate it," he repeated; and she understood that, used to power, he believed against all evidence that his hands, if only they were stronger and younger, could have held onto the chain, reburied the stake into the stone, saved the Mayor.

The events of the day flashed through her mind. This long, astounding day. "The fates took over, I expect," she told him, for what else could explain such a day?

"The fates? What fates?" he said furiously.

"The bad luck," she explained. "It came in threes, just the way they say. Being sick, you know, the guns at the airport, and now the chain breaking."

The Chairman chose to ignore this analysis. "Holy God, what a country!" he now said fervently. "Bob must be nuts to want to build a factory here."

"The cheap labour, I guess," offered Beth. She was, she realized, still breathing heavily. Her eyes felt hard and bright, as though her fever had returned. "Perhaps it will help them," she added automatically and wondered how it was she cared so little. Victims everywhere...but not her.

Below them the Mayor was being lifted, then placed in the back of the bus, loaded in like an old mattress.

"Poor bastard. How can you help in a place like this?" The Chairman jerked his head at the hut behind them. "Look at this joint. Madness!"

Exasperation shot through her. What was he talking about? Reason was madness, not this. This was natural...the violent country, the temples erected to cruelty, even the Mayor's accident. Couldn't the Chairman understand? The thing was that they were safe, he and she. Survivors. This time. By luck or good management, it didn't matter. She felt the stone pressing into her thighs and buttocks as reminder.

"It's perfectly natural," she told him, in a voice so different from her usual tone that he glanced sharply at her. At once she felt she had answered some never-expressed question. The Chairman decided she had snapped under the strain. Natural indeed!

She didn't go on, but she could have. Betrayal and death were natural, she could have added. So were pain and sickness and, perhaps, the transitory nature of love as well. She felt all this like a release, the breaking of bonds.

Below them people moved in aimless circles. She thought she spotted the Mayor's wife, the spiky-haired guide, the company men. One of those figures must surely be her husband. From here she couldn't be certain—he was so small—and of course it didn't really matter. The minibus was pulling slowly away from the crowd of people.

"You realize we're going to have to climb down from here," said the Chairman. He looked at her, his glinting old eyes full of another message. I'm frightened, I'm old, I'm going to die. "Climb down," he insisted. Help, said his eyes. A man can't admit his fear. You do it.

But Beth glanced away. She felt enshrined in her new, priestlike indifference. His voice barely reached her. "I suppose so," she said. I should feel sorry for him, she thought reluctantly, and for the Mayor too, but she was unable to remember even how sympathy felt. Since these things hadn't happened to her, it seemed now that they had hardly happened at all. A moment of drama, today's measure of excitement and the exhilaration fading already. Beside her the muttering Chairman seemed like a bothersome little child sent with her on a journey.

But then she had another thought. Perhaps this absence of pain was ephemeral, not to be counted upon. What if returning to earth she should slip into the old submissive mask again, resume the stupid, impotent posture of pain that she had shed. Climbing, she had cast it off. Or the Mayor falling had ripped it from her, or the heat and the magic tea, the guns and the fever. Who knew? Her gaze flew like an uncaged bird out across the tree tops, beyond the temples to the edge of the jungle, and on and on into the endless sky.

The Chairman wasn't sure at what instant she had risen to her feet. Only suddenly she was standing just ahead of him on the first step.

"Hey wait," he began. "We've got to…" She inclined her head back toward him, and he saw that she was smiling.

"In a minute," she told him in a tolerant distant voice, and turned away again. From his seat all he could see of her face now was the angelic curve of her cheek, her chin raised like a diver on the edge of perfection or disaster and the only certainty the dive itself.

About the Author

Julie Keith was born and raised near Chicago. After graduation from Smith College, she lived in Boston before moving to Montreal in 1965. At various times, Keith has worked in a bank and a brewery, and taught high school English. She has two children and three stepchildren. She lives in a tall old house in Montreal with her husband Richard Pound and a cat named Margaret .

Keith has four times been shortlisted in the CBC Literary Contest. Her stories have appeared in the anthologies *Souvenirs: New Fiction from Quebec* and *32 Degrees.* She has also been widely published in literary magazines, including *Canadian Fiction Magazine, Fiddlehead,* and *event. The Jaguar Temple and Other Stories* is Keith's first collection of short stories.